The Ballad

of

Desiree

Susan Carr

Table of Contents

Back Logging Roads of Idaho   1

The Pow-wow   7

The Tee-pee   10

Highway 2 and Hobo A#1   16

Spokaloo   19

The Greenhouse Cafe   21

Fruitland, Washington   24

The Sweat Lodge   31

The Chevy Van Returns   33

Sisterhood   39

Lake Roosevelt   44

The Huckleberry Mountains   49

Nesting   52

The Return   54

Day by Day   56

A Change   58

On My Own Again   59

Monogamy   61

A Fresh Start   63

The Midwife   65

The Birth   67

Family 70

Coyote 72

Leaving Fruitland 75

Center of the Universe - Fremont 76

Sisterhood 78

A Wedge 81

Mothers 83

Our Home 87

Friends 88

Men 90

My Audition 93

Raising Coyote 96

Strong Choices 99

Search and Rescue 101

The Test 103

Universal Mothers 106

The Boyfriend 108

The Picnic 110

My Birthday Wish 112

Wishes Do Come True 115

A Chance 118

Ruby's Choices 120

A Climb To The Top 125

Artists 129

Let's Party!	131
A Full Moon	133
Building A Home	137
The Move	139
The Learning School	140
A Teacher	145
The Singer	147
More Bands	150
Loving Coyote	153
Daily Life	156
A Respect for Acting	159
Ruby Clouds	163
Back in Fruitland	164
Musical Thoughts	168
The Huckleberry Hills	172
Hunting Honey	177
My Bed	179
Humming with the Hummingbirds	182
Peaches and Cream	184
A Pleasant Surprise	185
Emerson Cove	188
Mary's Store	191
Los Angeles	194
Fixing Fruitland	198

Visiting	200
More Choices	204
Stay Immersed	206
Keep Breathing	208
The Talk	212
A Family Meeting	216
A Decision	219
Coyote's Decision	225
ACKNOWLEDGMENTS	227
AUTHOR'S BIO	228

Back Logging Roads of Idaho

It's a large pale green 1949 Chevy van with paneled windows all around the back. The front seat smells of sweating leather.

The back logging roads of Idaho are a great pastime for a young girl of twenty-two in 1976. My Indian sun-skirt billows above my sweating thighs on this hot summer day.

"No bra for me!" My supple breasts do flip-flops under my gauzy linen top. My two dogs, Laddie and Sam, are panting in the back of the truck.

"What more does a girl need?" I sing happily as I turn the corner sharply. Down the gravel road, I spot a swaggering bare-chested man.

"Long hair," I murmur. "WHOOO girl." The sweat drips down my thighs to the leather below.

"My radiator is running empty at just the right time." I honk and pull over. The man with steel blue eyes just stops and stares.

"Kind of slow to react," I say. "Ooh, those Paul Newman eyes!"

I grab my rawhide pouch of filtered water to replenish my old jalopy's thirst. I open up the hood and climb onto the front fender. I pry open the radiator cap, and begin filling the head of the radiator. I conjure up wild images of the bare-chested man admiring how the wind can gently brush over my ass and slightly sway my short sun-skirt. I imagine a smile of admiration as he rocks side to side in his cowhide boots. As he approaches, I hold my breath. I chuckle slightly as I tighten the radiator cap on. In the spur of the moment, I jump off and fall back against his bare-chest.

"Oooh, excuse me!" as I flash my full smile directly to his eyes. He returns the gesture. I feel this intense energy coming from him and entering my body. It takes my breath away. Laddie and Sam nudge their noses on my legs.

"Want a ride?"

He nods.

Oh boy! Girl, have you got your day cut out for you. I head back over to the driver's side and jump in. He throws his pack into the back of the van, but I hear Sam growling. I have always loved Sam for being my protector. Vince, my old music teacher gave him to me. Apparently when Sam was born, his master beat him and broke his spirit. But now he is mine and anytime a man approaches me, he make sure not to welcome him.

"Down Sam!" I shout as the man gets into the passenger side. "Hey! Let me show you one of my favorite watering holes."

I start up the old rig and off we bump down the old gravel road.

"There's a place up ahead that I love to go to. Legend has it that many maidens came to cleanse and dress themselves there for ceremonial use. You from around here?"

He just shrugs no.

I want to say, 'Cat got your tongue?' But I just fix my eyes on his golden-bronze body and long, brown hair. There are bits of leaves and twigs in it as though he has been traveling in the woods and not the main road.

I become flush from the heat and my thighs

tingle from looking at him. Around the bend, I see large boulders and can hear the rush of the river. I gear down and turn to the right into a flat meadow.

"Here it is!" I open the door and hop down. I take off my sandals immediately, so that my feet can feel the soft mossy ground. I walk a little ways towards my favorite boulder. Taking off my skirt and top, I climb on to this rock that is so smooth. The granite feels warm against my youthful skin.

"Funny," I chuckle. "He's still in the truck."

I close my eyes and nestle my spine against the heat of the granite. Dozing off for a few minutes, I awaken to hear splashing in the water. Either it is the dogs or him. I open one eye and glance towards the sound. There he is.

"Now does he have any stitch of clothing on?" I ponder.

Soon he glides over to another rock and gently lifts his full bare-ass to me.

"Ah!" I sigh. As he rolls his tan body over, I notice something catching the sunlight. It is a ruby in his navel.

Wow! Ouuwie, fiery red, exciting me. His eyes catch mine.

"My name is Ruby." he says breaking his silence.

My eyes gleam with admiration. His head drops back slowly to the granite and he dozes off. Without missing a beat, my head settles back too. Maybe an hour has gone by when my stomach begins to growl and I wake quickly. He is still there sleeping like a baby. I climb down and dip my baking body into the refreshing waters. Suddenly I spot a coyote sniffing my clothes and holler. Sam and Laddie start yelping and the bare-chested man - or rather Ruby - jumps in after me. I start throwing rocks fearing that Sam and the coyote might have it out. As I take a long throw, my arm nearly hits Ruby. He is standing right next to me in waist- deep waters. The coyote, startled by all this commotion, takes off.

"Good Sam!" I yell. Tilting my head to the right, I take my damsel in distress pose.

"Are you alright?" Ruby takes my hand.

"Oh yes. Thank you."

"I didn't want you to get hurt." He guides me out of the river. While I gather up my clothes, I realize that Ruby is a gentle man.

"Let's be on our way." I say.

He grabs my Panama straw hat and places it upon his brow. I hold my tongue at such a bold act!

Heading towards the truck, I jump in and start it up. Cranking once, twice, but on the third time, the starter doesn't want to kick over.

"Shit," I whisper as my efforts prove to be futile. Something is definitely wrong. But, Ruby is nowhere in sight. In fact, he is trying to make friends with Sam. That's sweet. Maybe mechanical figuring-outs aren't his thing. Oh well, I never could lasso a handy, white knight in shining armor.

"Well, we might have to hitch-hike out of here. There's a town close by; maybe we can replace the old ticker in this thing."

Ruby and I put our thumbs out, and hit the hot dusty road.

The dogs take off in front of us as we slowly meander our way around the bend.

"So, where are you going?" I say.

"I'm like the bank over there, just watching what the river will bring by."

"Nah! You are not on this same road every day

wondering who's going to pick you up. Are you?"

"I do believe you picked me up. And why did you?"

"Maybe it was your Paul Newman eyes. Did anyone ever tell you, you have Paul Newman eyes?"

"No, only you. Where are you going?"

"Me, I'm just on a drive. Sometimes I get in my old truck and take off. I don't look at a map or set a destination. I like to be rambling to whatever comes along, whatever road stands in my way. I do have a place, a cabin in Fruitland. It's a beautiful place, twenty acres tucked into the foothills of the Huckleberry Mountains. Where's your home?"

"Wherever I lay my bed. I'm not attached to anyone or anything. Just randomly living each day. That's me."

"It must be kind of peaceful to not have much care in the world. Watching the seasons of life go by and living each day just for today, not yesterday or tomorrow. You know, you are sort of 'present' only for this moment in time. I like that, I do. Me, I like to settle in a 'nesting' situation for a while. You're a Gypsy, aren't you?"

"You might say."

"Wow, I've always wanted to meet a Gypsy. Where have you been?"

Suddenly, a car varooms up the road behind us. It is a white Cadillac with a huge set of cow horns fastened on its front end.

"Wow, a Texas ranger! Hey!" I start waving my gingham handkerchief. The driver obviously sees my distress signal and pulls over.

"You need a ride?" an old gray-haired man in a silver auctioneer outfit asks. I like his ivory bolo with a hunk of turquoise in the center.

5

"Certainly. We had some truck problems about a mile or so back."

"Oh yea! I saw your vehicle. Well, I'm headed toward the Indian pow-wow up near Harrison. Why don't you sit in the back, girlie and your friend up-front."

I whistle for the dogs. They jump in. As I slide in, my ass has quite a sensation. Man, the best! Cool, soft, cushy white leather. My ass appreciates such a pleasure.

Then I notice the old man adjusting his mirror a little lower to the right. Well, I know that if you're lowering and shifting, you must want to be looking at something. Men have always been attracted to me. Maybe cause I have had a full-figured body since an early age. My breasts are large, so large that I can be standing looking down to the floor and I can't see my feet. I am also not shy about my body. I dress and ornate it in any fabric or style I chose. Many look mainly because I am not concerned with how much I reveal.

"So partner, is this your old lady?"

"Well yeah, as a matter of fact she is," boasts the bare-chested man.

A slight grin hits my face when I notice the man quickly adjusting his mirror back again. But there is a slight warmth in my heart at the thought of being Ruby's old lady.

"Well, where are you both heading to?"

I start to speak but I notice Ruby enjoys taking over the conversation as if it is the manly thing to do. I think I will just sit back and enjoy the air-conditioning blowing on my face and under my skirt. Looking out the back-window, I wonder what the pow-wow would be like.

The Pow-wow

The horn honks and the motion of the car takes an extreme right. My body is knocked over to the car door and I awaken.

"Whoa." The front doors fly open. "Have I been asleep for awhile?"

Ruby and the old auctioneer are out of the Cadillac talking to the gas attendant. It sounds like my mental message of the pow-wow has been received loud and clear by Ruby. They are asking how to get there. I hop out of the back seat to hit the girl's room and buy some snacks for the trip. I pass by the gas station attendant. He nods his head and watches me closely as I open the squeaky screen door of the Last Stop Gas Mart. Oh, what shall I get for the boys? Potato chips, orange soda and some Oreos.

"Anything else for you, honey?" The old lady at the counter looks up.

"No. Thank you very much," I say as I lay down some cash.

I look out the window and notice the bare-chested Ruby is now covered up. The air conditioning must have got to him. Probably good for the old lady who runs this store, she might have dropped over dead or had a swooning faint.

"Is the pow-wow far from here?" getting her attention.

"No honey, it's just up the road to the left, up in the foot-hills there. Going to be a great week-end for it."

"Thanks!"

As I swing open the screen door, howling dogs

7

and honking horns beckon for my return.

"Here, got some snacks for the road trip."

"Hope you don't mind," Ruby turns to greet me. "I'd like to go to the pow-wow. I have a strange feeling there is someone there I need to meet."

"No problem, Ruby. I'd love to see what the Great Spirit has to say."

The auctioneer takes no time to barrel his Cadillac down the road, slipping and sliding against the loose gravel.

"There's some trading I need to do up there too," butts in the auctioneer. "I got some deals in the making; you know the turquoise business."

"I thought so. You sure have a beautiful bolo."

"Thanks, my wife got it for me in a little town in New Mexico."

"Sounds romantic!"

"Yeah, she was one hunk of a good woman. She passed away one year ago."

"Oh, sorry." I realize I have gone too far and opened a sore wound. "Man, the terrain here is different than where I come from. Your trees look more evergreen and denser. Not like our tamaracks and tumbleweeds. Must be some great fishing in those lakes."

Soon I can see rows and rows of tee-pees and scores and scores of old trucks and four-doors lined up and entering past the gate of a great celebration. I hear lots of drumming and see signs for fry bread, crafts, smoked fish, and the famous stick games. The tee-pees number in the fifties and the women are all decked out in their squaw skirts and braided hair.

"Let me out!" I shout.

We pick a spot to park and out we jump. Laddie and Sam find some companions to roam with. The auctioneer waves down some old fat fart. Ruby leans against the Cadillac. He just stares at me as I gather up my belongings.

"Ruby is certainly a man of few words," I say to myself.

The Tee-pee

It is so magical: the drumming, the swirling of colorful skirts and clanging of rattles on the dresses, everything intensifies as each tribe tries to out-do the other in the dance competitions. The sun is starting to set. Soon large bon-fires are roaring as the male dancers take to center stage. Intense bidding is going on in the 'stick game' corner. People are yelling back and forth to each other. I have no idea what is going on. I stand for a long time and close my eyes. I take several deep breaths and then I feel the presence of Ruby behind me.

"They're gambling. They're showing the sticks and then they're not showing them. They're betting on how many there are. They're egging each other on to guess wrong."

"Oh." I feel his warm breath separate the strands of my hair. It is amazing to be in the trance of the game, hearing the drums, the singing and dancing. Oh, my mind is spinning.

"Here, I have something for you."

Ruby hands me what looks like a cup of water.

"My friend I told you about said we could stay in his tee-pee."

"Yeah, I need to rest awhile," I start to sip. "It has a bitter and sweet taste to it."

"It's peyote tea with some honey. It will help replenish your spirit."

"Pee-yoo-tee, what a lovely word. Pee-yoo-tee."

My body starts to move to the drums and I want to press myself so close to Ruby as if I could climb inside his skin.

"Come," Ruby summons. "Let's go to the tee-pee."

I follow like any lap dog. Who wouldn't at this point? I want to take off all my clothes right there and then. But Ruby I guess is sort of a conservative, a modest type of guy.

As we approach the front flap of the tee-pee, the music pulsates with heightened excitement as the male and female dancers release their cries.

Inside the tee-pee is an open fire pit and a large Indian blanket for two. My shirt is already off and I take no time to stand inches from my bare-chested man. Ruby's energy and mine are mixed as I crawl inside his skin. All that remains is the shadows of our bodies against the buck-skinned fortress, dancing.

I awaken. The smell of hot coffee and fry-bread dripping with honey is laid out before me. My hand is cupped between my legs and sunrise is streaking through the cracks of the tee-pee. Ruby is nowhere in sight but what a gentlemen to bring me breakfast in bed.

My body needs no clothing, for the warmth of the day is already beginning. When I am done savoring the last piece of sweet dough, the auctioneer taps on the outside flap of the tee-pee entrance.

"Missus, Ruby gave me this to give you. Are you awake?"

I take my sun skirt and hold it loosely in front of my body as my hand reaches out for the letter.

"Thanks, Mr. Auctioneer. Hope your trading is going well!"

"Well, it is ma'am, really, really well."

I close the flap and sit down on the Indian blanket still damp from last evening's episode. The letter is addressed to no one. For it is true, I have never given Ruby my name. Inside read:

> *My friend must leave and I will follow with him.*
> *There is nothing to be alarmed about.*
> *Last night leaves my mind and soul wanting*
> *to return to you...*
> *your spirit is inside me*
> > *Ruby*

"Oh by the way, Missus," the auctioneer trumpets forth with his eyes admiring my backside. "Ruby's friend gave you his Camaro."

"A Camaro? You have got to be kidding."

"Here the keys!" the auctioneer says ending the conversation.

Alone in the tee-pee, I look up at the poles reaching to the blue sky and finish dressing.

"Let's go, dogs! It's time to head home."

I open the flap of the tee-pee and sitting larger than life is a two-door 1976 white Camaro with black interior. God, I cannot believe this car. This must be the funniest joke, to see me sitting in a white Camaro with my two hounds shedding all over the back end. Well, beggars can't be choosy. But a Palomino would have suited me better.

Starting the V8 engine, I feel a little loud in this car, or maybe it is the muffler half-torn off by the deep potholes in the road. But it is a way to get back to my rig, so off I rumble. Noticing the gas gauge is near empty, I head back out to the gas station again.

Like a roadster from hell, I stop to get supplies for the trip back. To my delight, a 1949 gray Chevy pick-up with a shingled house on its bed is parked in front.

Man, what a beauty. I've always wanted a house on the back-end. Getting out of the sleek Camaro, I go inside the gas station. Inside, a young man with mousy brown locks is paying his bill.

"Hey Mister! Is that your truck outside?"

"Yeah, it certainly is. Why?" he asks as he turns around to face me. "You need some help?"

"Well, yes I do. I've got a 1949 green Chevy paneled van not far from here. I thought since both of us are familiar with these kinds of trucks, you might be able to help me figure out a small problem I'm having with it."

"I don't mind."

"Great! Let me get my two dogs."

"Wow! Is that your car? That white 1976 Camaro. Man I love those cars. I'm heading for California and I'd love to drive down in a white Camaro. Are the tires in good shape?"

"Well yes, I think so. Why don't you start it up and see how you like it. In fact, why don't I give you the white Camaro in exchange for you helping me on my van."

"Sounds fair."

"Lordly, that would be so great."

"Let's leave the Camaro here and go check out your van."

"OK. Sam and Laddie, in the back."

Jumping up on the side step of his Chevy, I swing my legs onto the same sweating leather my ass has grown so well to love.

This fella I am traveling with is a pretty talkative sort. He is kind of straight ahead. In fact, he loves to sing. He has a guitar in the front. On the way to my broken down van, he teaches me the Kookaburra song:

Kookaburra sits in the old gum tree
Merry, merry king of the bush is he
Laugh Kookaburra! Laugh Kookaburra!
Gay your life must be.

We sing in rounds and just laugh our heads off about animals we admire. He is quite the musician. We make up lyrics and melodies. He is a pretty happy-go-lucky kind of guy. Why he wants to go to California in a white Camaro, that I can't figure out. But he makes me laugh all the way up those back logging roads to my old jalopy.

When we arrive, my sweet baby is sitting there just as we left her. He is quite amazed at the old rig and her upkeep.

"Lots of love went into her."

"Yeah and I get lots back."

He opens up her front end and checks the inners of her working mechanics. Clinking, checking and clanking, he starts her up and adjusts, twists and pulls all the possible possibilities of her system.

"Well, she's an old one, she is. I think she might need to go back into town to see a friend of mine. He could really solve some deeper problems that she has."

"Well, that's OK with me if I have a way back to my place. Maybe if I let you have the Camaro for California, you could let me have your pickup?"

"No problem. Here's my mechanic's name and number. He'll call you when your van's ready."

"And when you get back, you could stay awhile at my place in Fruitland and we could write some more tunes together."

"Sounds like a regular deal. So here's the keys."

"And here's the keys to the Camaro. You take

care of yourself and let me know how things are going for you, business and all. Yeah, just write me at Desiree, Fruitland, Washington. It always gets to me, but wait! How will you sign it?"

"Big Paul Skinny!"

I give him a big kooka bear hug to wish him on his way. And I do think I'll see that Big Paul Skinny again. I wave goodbye as he heads off in my old van to start his new life in the Camaro.

As I start up his truck, I feel like I am being two-faced to my old van. I have had her for such a long time. She has carried the goats and dogs to the fairgrounds. Sometimes I fill the back end with hay and the goats, dogs, and me and curl up together to take a nap. She is like my home away from home. Now I'd be stepping out for a new truck with a house on the back. The dogs are certainly happy though.

There is a small loft where they can sit high up to watch the scenery of great pines and tamaracks towering by. The day is starting off fine as we curve around the bend to Spokaloo. Maybe some lunch at the Greenhouse Cafe to see Skip, Salty and Dave and that sweet sister Suzanne.

Thinking about Big Paul Skinny, I start a new song:

> *Love and the road keep on bending*
> *And it won't be too long*
> *The sound of your voice*
> *Will be bringing me home*

Highway 2 and Hobo A#1

As the hours unfold with me singing the Kookaburra song, I spot an old hobo with wild gray hair bushed out looking for a ride on Highway 2. Certainly this man has some stories to tell and will help me pass the time. I toot and slow down to stop. Lowering the passenger window, I start to open my mouth when into the cab drifts...

> "*You are the meadow of the unicorn*
> *You are exploding flowers*
> *Sing, sing, sing, sing...*"

"Well, I have been singing, so why don't you come with me and we'll start a duet or something?" I sing back.

> "*I am an astrolabe*
> *and no navigator at all...*"

"Well, hell, I know my way around these parts so I'll be your navigator, old man." I reply.

> "*You are the constellations, the stars and the planets*
> *You are the unseen points of light logic...*"

"You are certainly long winded." I chuckle.

> "*Logic has no knowledge*
> *O Rainbow, O Rainbow, O Rainbow...*"

"Well no one has ever called me Rainbow. That's certainly a compliment. I'm heading for lunch in Spokaloo at the Greenhouse Cafe. Can I give you a ride there?"

"Yes."

And at my request he jumps right in the cab to share the last leg of my adventure towards civilization.

He's an interesting man, with gray thick hair down to his shoulders. You know I love men with thick hair and the longer the better. Kind of like a horse with good teeth. Exotic. Always starts a rush inside of me. The older the better has always been my philosophy. They have more knowledge and wisdom of the world. This one isn't going to disappoint me.

"You rolling in off the train from somewhere, Mister Hobo?" I inquire.

> *"A crumbly, rumply walk*
> *Down by an abandoned railroad track..."*

"Yep, that was what I thought."

> *"I love the bite of ballast on my shoes..."*

"You know, me too, I love walking. I've done plenty of it in the last few days."

> *"I've been working on the railroad so nothing*
> *much matters to me. What's another festival*
> *to a man with two paydays a month? It does*
> *seem suddenly awkward that I do not have a*
> *name comfortably to call you. I should invent*
> *one or perhaps you should, or we should..."*

"Well, there's only one name for me. Desiree. And as for you, I'll invent one for you."

> *"A sorting out of desires, a centering?*
> *Desiree, desiring, your wishes, fancy fantasy,*

Put your mind to it. Are you willing?
Eager?"

"And you, shall I call you, Hemmingway, Yeats or Shelley?" Creating a sudden pause in our conversation.

"A Number 1."

Spokaloo

There it was. Me and A#1 off to the Greenhouse Cafe for lunch. Maybe some creamy jalapenos or buckwheat pancakes or plum pudding. There is beauty everywhere today. The sun is out, the lush golden wheat fields are waving their heads in the slight mid-morning breeze. And I am singing new melodies with new poetry. Sitting next to me is this famous hobo, Hobo A#1. His signature is written on every red brick wall and under old railroad bridges all around these parts. Hobo A#1 is a talented man with words of poetry that need to be spoken or sung. Under the bridges his poetry is written and tucked behind loose bricks. Poetry written for the masses. You have to be chosen, and I have, by Hobo A#1.

> *Black starling*
> *Bullfrog song*
> *Listen to your sisters*
> *Everyone will suspect your mother of mad love*
> *Love your bullfrog song*
> *But I am mad and free.*

The mid-day heat reaches the mid-90's or so and my mouth is watering for a Dos Equis. Swinging right down Division Street, past the Red Lion BBQ, I signal across three lanes of lunchtime traffic and park my new truck under a little shade. Hobo A #1 is wide-eyed and bushy-tailed.

"Perhaps we can walk through the city or the country and talk to each other, find things and see them

and turn them into words and into music...no....songs...that's the word...music is big like art...and is harder to talk about."

"Hold on, my friend, my stomach is churning with thunderous sounds. I have got to eat. No more songs today."

I am out-walking him by a half of a block and as I turn, he keeps mumbling sounds and continues towards a bridge by the Spokane River.

"Sure you don't want some cornbread? What? Need to find me? Desiree, Fruitland. Write me. Write me in the morning. I will be home. Write me..." I holler, and wave farewell.

"It is really good to have someone to make words for..." I faintly hear him say.

"Bye, Hemmingway...What an odd man, surely a friend, a platonic friend." I blow him a kiss.

The Greenhouse Cafe

The screen door slams and the reality bug bites me.
FOOD! Got to have it now. I swing open the green
door. And right in the middle of Al Green and the
bustling chattering patrons, I roar my "Ahooooo!"
like a coyote. All the sisters come running out to
greet me, "AHOOOOOO!" Hugs and kisses, slaps on
the back, the love that only women can keep giving.
Sister Suzanne, her apron wrung by her strong
hands, grabs me.

"Girl, where you've been? I've got your
favorite."

"Oh my, my. Creamy jalapenos tostadas?
Whoopee!" I toss my Panama hat into the ceiling fan.
"You knew I'd be back. So what the news, sister
Suzanne?"

"Well..." sister Suzanne snaps her fingers and a
younger sister comes out with a turkey platter-sized
plate of my favorite dish.

We sit in the corner amongst the palm trees and
sister Suzanne's homegrown ten-foot avocado tree.

With long, Rapunzel locks, always glittering
gold below her small perky tits, sister Suzanne
dresses like a Gypsy. Her see-through sun shirt
absorbs the warmth of the sun and of men. A couple
of years ago, she came stumbling in one morning
with a pack on her back, tin cans clattering her
arrival. She was parched and had been hitchhiking a
long distance to get somewhere. She landed on the
front porch of the Greenhouse Cafe at 6:30 a.m. I was
the main cook that day unlocking the door to all my
male customers.

I wasn't surprised to see this sister. The Greenhouse is a magnet to all lost sisters trying to make a place for themselves. The screen door always is open for adventurous types. There she was, asking for food, water, and a chance to make a buck. I gave her a broom and set her to work. She watched me knead thirty brown loaves of bread for lunchtime fixings. At breakfast, she saw me flipping buckwheat pancakes, and smothering my very favorite omelettes with deep purple huckleberries sauce.

Big mugs of coffee started our days. Al Green serenading our moves, and a place where women threw in just the right touch for a man. Suzanne and I started singing our hearts out, she sweeping and washing the pots and plates by hand and getting ready for the next bunch of beautiful men to grace our tables.

"The Red Lion BBQ had their big race just last week and everybody missed you, Desiree. Remember last year?" Suzanne brings me back to the present.

"Yeah," I am laughing really hard. "Me and what's his name?"

We had to get to the Red Lion about 9 a.m., bikes and all. At 10 a.m., the race started. Always during the Lilac Festival, Eddie the bartender cranks up a big barrel hot with coals for pig and beefy ribs and beans and fried bread with honey. About one hundred people gather for the race. You first have to sign your life away, get a bike and as soon as you hear the gunshot, you take off riding. You hit every bar that is on your treasure map. The bartender gives you a playing card and a schooner of beer and off you ride to your next destination. But the distances covers a lot of territory and as each beer settles in, you look sillier and sillier riding your bike.

"Yeah, what's his name and I looked like laugh-in contestants, falling off our bikes and barely making the finish line. But we had a great time, puke and all."

"Well, there was just more of it. Puke, that is," sister Suzanne giggles. She gets up, and heads for the kitchen. "You staying the night?"

"Sure, my sweet sister."

Fruitland, Washington

"Fruitland girls! Just 80 miles away. Come Sam and Laddie! In the back."

Traveling up old Highway 2, taking a right near Davenport, then onto Highway 25 to Egypt and Miles. There is nothing prettier than these roads. Vast lands of wheat, alfalfa and barley waving back and forth by God's great hands. Old homesteads, creakity barns and packs of coyotes watching as the tumbleweeds mosey on by. Grain, gold tipped, green cedar-trees and the rustling wind. A sky so high that stacks of clouds float by into shapes for your guessing. Picturesque to my eyes to only to a few others that have seen God's country.

My cabin is straight up from the Spokane Indian reservation. Take a right at Fruitland's Bible camp. Around the bend there is the smell of cows and as you take a left by the willow tree you see the beaver's camp. Better slow down; the washboard road will rattle the screws out of any old jalopy. Around another bend, pass a yellow house there are rows of mailboxes welcoming you to the Huckleberry Mountains. My road. Eyeing my hollowed out log mailbox, I spy a letter.

"Whoopee!" I holler as I slam on the brakes and back into reverse. I reach out my left arm to pluck my correspondence. Ripping open the left side of this envelope reveals no return address, just:

> *Desiree*
> *Fruitland, WA*

Inside:

Desiree
You think that I would leave without knowing
who you are
I am not that way
As a leaf falls into the river with the change of
the season
Another drops to accompany it, to find its
way.
I will return to you soon
My blood brother needs me.
He will send word of me
Look for a man with a tattoo on his arm, a
blue heron.
  Ruby, your inner soul

I turn the motor off and sit just looking at the afternoon sun and its glorious rays baking my body.

"Ruff, ruff." Laddie and Sam jump out of the back of the truck and run straight ahead, no stopping, just run past the Gramer's to our homestead. Lord, I better get them before they get into trouble again. Cows, pigs, horses, chickens, you name it. Anything that's got legs on it and can run, they love to chase. Laddie is there just for the fun of it. Sam is who I'm nervous for. He's got that twinkle in his eye that means only one thing: KILLER.

Around to the right, I can see Rachael Gramer running after her horses. She's got a 2 X 4 in her hand thinking she's going to knock some sense into them. Sam is sniffing trouble with Rachael and barking like crazy.

"Sam, shut up!"

Rachael looks up. She and her family seem like thick people, dense, not much up in the head. Her family lives in an old homestead situated by the Orapakan creek. They've got pigs, cows, kids, whatever, sitting in their creek, 24 hours a day. Their laundry is always flapping in the wind and God only knows that eight children create a lot of it. They've got a TV and a telephone but the inside of the house reminds me of an Appalachian family. Cook-stove covered with pig and cow grease, a kitchen filled with boxes of cereal, bags of potato chips, open Schlitz beer cans and children with wide-eyes and pasty skin. There are a few who wear overalls with one strap secured and are always walking bare-foot. With their short-cropped marine hair-dos they look in-bred. The friendly neighbor look never comes my way, but just a 'look and a nod!'

Sam hears my voice and comes running beside the truck as we turn up our road. The road is a secret and so over-grown that no one knows it's there. Brittle knap weed covers the first half of the road until you pass the rusty remains of a mill saw and a pink tractor. Wild rose bushes choke the old insides of these engines. There are fruit trees that have never been taken care of as well, but a little ways further is an open field. This is the best part. Sometimes a red fox or a baby black bear crosses our path and we chase it towards the pond, up through a growth of salmonberries and tamaracks and then to a large field where my cabin sits.

I bought this place on my own. My ma died early in her life and she left me with some money. I had no home and I needed one. I didn't need a man to buy it. Land was cheap so I bought it and built my cabin. It is octagonal, eight sides with Douglas firs stack tight and an eight-foot Douglas stump standing as the hub of the wheel in the middle of the house.

The stump is three foot in diameter. It secures the two floors.

Everything about the place is salvage. The floors are oak pallets that I found outside a piano store in Spokaloo. I sanded them down and puttied them together one by one. There's a ladder connecting the first floor to the second. The second floor is where my bedroom is. As you slide open the bedroom door, you can see the floor is covered by a patched work quilt rug of blue, green, brown and beige remnant scraps. In my bedroom there are two hanging plants, and several mobiles of found objects of feathers, beads, sticks and shells. There is a batik on the wall, scented candles on top of a built-in shelf, a bed on the floor and my grandmother's chest of drawers with a mirror on top. Across from my bedroom is an crawl space for storage and another bunk loft for an unexpected traveler.

Below, on the first floor, is a large open living room with two rockers, an upright cherry wood piano, and a kitchen with tiles that were repainted with sailing ships and setting suns within a landscape of the Huckleberry Mountains.

My favorite room is my bathroom. No toilet. It's outside. There is a small wash sink with wood paneling, a large bathtub, and a window to look out of with a green painted frame.

Everywhere in the cabin there is light that shines through salvaged windows. Cathedral ceilings and two wood stoves keep it warm through the chilly nights of winter. It is my sacred place, where I play my Erick Satie piano music late into the night while the smell of kerosene fills the air.

The dogs are hungry but so is Sweet Chariot, my horse.

She is a Palomino and she is grunting to get some sweet oats. The dogs are starting to open up a big bag of chow as I feed Sweet Chariot. After I do some bonding with Sweet Chariot I gather up some kindling and paper to light a fire. Taking off my tan suede cowboy boots and tossing my hat on the antler horns, I sit watching the sun starting to set on the horizon. Closing my eyes, I breathe in the beauty of this place. It is very peaceful here, with no phones or TV, just silence. A good kind of life, the kind that says you're connected.

Dozing off for a moment, I begin to hear the coyotes yelping in the hills above. It seems there's one a little louder than the others. My ears perk up, as the sound gets closer to the cabin. Funny it's just one, not the whole pack. Sam starts growling and Laddie starts howling and pretty soon what seemed to be the beginning of a restful sleep has been awaken to a roar of noise. Oh, oh! Got to get the rifle down and check what's going on. I definitely hear scratching around the outside logs, and footsteps heading around the back door.

"This coyote is a curious fella to be coming so close to me. Let's give him a scare, Sam and Laddie," I whisper. "Go!" I yell and reach to open the back door.

Suddenly a figure of a man jumps up right in front of the glass door. Wow! a gorgeous looking man. An Apache with long-black hair stands perfectly still.

"Whoa, whoa, I surrender," He says.

"Who are you?"

"Blue Heron. I'm a friend of Ruby's. In fact, I'm the one that took him away from you at the pow-wow. He said I'd find you here, so I came to make peace between us. I never have come between him and a woman before. He didn't want to leave. He wanted me to tell you."

"Well, boy, he certainly wants to make sure I'm OK with it. I got his letter today."

"That's why I came. Sometimes one can't trust the mail but it's different when a real person shows up. I also wanted to meet you. Ruby seems to be taken with you."

"Well, come on in."

He enters. He looks around my place being quite inquisitive.

"Did you build this yourself?"

"Yep, sure did. A lot of the folks on this mountain helped and the design was something I've always been partial to. It's..."

"Octagonal, eight-sided, almost like a circle. It is very magical. Much vibration. This is a good place with good medicine."

"Would you like some supper? I haven't eaten much all day."

"Certainly!"

There is something about this man that makes me feel like he is connected to me in a way of the heart. As I start to make dinner he listens and speaks with passion and fire, like someone who has too much piss and vinegar.

When the meat is ready and the beets all boiled, we sit down together, candles lit, and exchange laughter and tears. He is easy. He occasionally leaves to go outside with the bats and smoke his American Spirits. I watch him from the window as he looks up and sees the stars and the spectacle of the big Milky Way. I feel accepted on another level with him. When he comes back in, he announces he will stay and rightly so, for he has become my friend also.

I fix him a place with bedding, pillows and thick blankets. He is appreciative.

"Tomorrow, I will make you a sweat."

"A sweat? Why, that would be great. Haven't experienced that yet."

We part, me upstairs and him below.

The Sweat Lodge

About sunrise, I awake to chopping, the smell of a fire getting started, and sounds of rocks crackling in a pit. Blue Heron has taken some willow branches and bent them into the shape of a semi-circle and has covered it with blankets he collected from inside for the top. Inside the hut is a round hole where the rocks are. I am told to bring water from the creek nearby. When I return he has already taken off his shirt. So I start to take off mine.

"No, you must wear a skirt and a top. We enter the sweat spiritually with no distractions."

Modesty? I'm thinking to myself. This is the first time a man's been wanting me to be modest. Well, why not? Another new experience.

We enter the hut, in silence. After he closes the entrance, he begins to chant and sing in a language that is not familiar to me. He has a beautiful voice. Quite strong and majestic. My thoughts go deep inside myself to a place of comfort and warmth and quiet. I am starting to fidget because of the immense heat. My forehead feels like it is on fire and my heart is starting to race. I feel like I can't get a deep enough breathe. I need to get out of here.

"Keep breathing, Desiree."

"Oh this is hard."

"I know, but you have it inside of you. Keep breathing and quiet your mind."

I am sweating and listening to his drum and trying to find my own drum. He chants for a long time and in between he throws water on the rocks for more heat intensity. I breathe deeply and lower my head to the cold ground because it has become unbearable. His chanting and drumming increases in volume and as I breathe down into my thighs my mind begins to control my fear of leaving. I am transported. He opens the flap for light and the morning air cools the insides. We leave quiet, each in our own personal solitude. I walk down the side of the hill to the creek because my clothes are drenched. I lay my body in the fast moving current to rinse away my toxins. My face feels soft and open. When I come back up the hill, Blue Heron has vanished.

The hut remains, with steam rolling off its backside. But nowhere do I see him.

"Too bad!" I say aloud, wishing we had more time to talk.

The dogs come running up from the road with happy grins on themselves.

"Gophers? Girls, I guess today makes us all feel so glad to be alive."

The Chevy Van Returns

A few days later, I am working out in the garden, picking beans off of a bush bean crop that is in seventh heaven. The horse manure must have been the right combination of nutrients because these bush beans are plentiful. More than I can consume in a year even if I did freeze or can them. I love working in the field, getting the soil underneath my fingertips and playing with the five- hearted earth-worms. Suddenly I hear what I think is my van coming up the road. But no, the sun must have me day dreaming.

"Well, we better take a stroll on down that road, girls!"

But before I can get ten feet, coming through the grove of wild roses is my van. There is a funny guy driving it and he is singing at the top of his lungs.

> "*Kookaburra sits in the old gum tree*
> *Merry merry king of the bush is he*
> *Laugh Kookaburra! Laugh Kookaburra!*
> *Gay your life must be...*"

Lord in heaven, oh thank you Lord. I am beaming from ear to ear as I see Mr. Big Paul Skinny. The old van clinks and clanks as he drives her up and parks her by the side of the cabin and jumps out.

"This here's your van, delivered safe and sound by Big Paul Skinny."

"Well, well, I am so astounded. You deliver too. How is she doing? And why aren't you in California?"

"Well, as my mother always said, life is full of a

number of things. But your van is doing fine. She hummed all the way over, never missing a beat. How are you, my sweet voice?"

"My, my," blushing to myself. "Well, Mister Big Paul Skinny..." I glance over and notice there is a guitar in the front seat. "Why don't you sing me some tunes while I finish working on my bush beans."

"Certainly, certainly."

Mister Big Paul Skinny isn't a tall man. He is about five foot nine. But I am partial to his long mousey brown hair flowing down to his shoulders and his moustache that hangs down low past the corners of his mouth. He has a beautiful voice that reminds me of long ago troubadours. I've never been serenaded before. But this is nice, real nice. I like it when men come courting.

> *"I can't live without your love*
> *Can't love without you in my life*
> *Can't be without your beauty*
> *Can't live without you in my heart*
> *O Desiree, My Desiree*
> *You are the daytime that wakes my night*
> *O Desiree, O my Desiree*
> *I am the arrow and you the flight"*

I join in with some harmonies as we both pick beans. He talks about heading on his great trip to the land of sunshine. He dreams of being a singer in a band and striking it rich. He likes my sweet voice and when the afternoon sun becomes intense, we saunter over into the cabin for some ice mint tea.

Big Paul Skinny knows how to make himself at home anywhere. He reminds me of a turtle with his house on its back. Always ready to go. Never leaving home because home is wherever he will be that night. He notices my piano in the living room and hops right over and plunks himself down.

"Oh, this is a beaut!"

"Yeah, my piano is my prize possession. When my grandma passed away she said I was the one to have it." I walk over to the piano and slide open a door that reveal a roller. "It's a player piano. Rolls and rolls of music she gave to me." I sit down next to him.

"See, you play it by pumping your feet below on the large metal petals. Kind of like walking, and the gears turn round and round as the paper with tiny little squares plays the piano keys. Pretty magical!"

I remember spending hours as a little girl just pumping away and listening to its honky-tonk sounds. It was mesmerizing to me as I saw the paper speak to the piano and it translating back melodies. I sang along just like Big Paul Skinny does now singing his heart out. I love to sing. It puts me in a different place. Quiet, alone, but fulfilled.

Growing up for me was a battleground of explosions, crashing and banging. Minefields of sound where you never could walk or talk. I couldn't be safe there. But I could be safe on that little piano bench down in the basement where a single light bulb listened to my voice and my feet kept walking through it all.

Big Paul Skinny starts to play some chords and hums a melody.

"Let's write a song together." I start to hold back.

"Cat got your tongue, Desiree?"

"I've never written much."

"Why?"

"Because I stuttered when I was little girl, Big Paul Skinny."

"Well, hell, all the great country singers stuttered. But when they sang, the words just flowed out effortlessly."

I began to scribble down some words.

The road keeps on bending
It won't be long
the feeling of your love
is bringing me home

"How about this?" Big Paul Skinny starts to sing and play.

"The road keeps on bending to the left and the right
Our song keeps on singing late into the night..."

I light the kerosene lamp and that's what we do. We keep singing late into the night. I am just finishing my last chords when my eyes catch a black flying thingamajig, whooping and swishing by me.

"Whoops, run for cover, Big Paul."

Big Paul Skinny starts leaping and ducking under the piano keys and I duck under the kitchen table. Gosh darn those bats again! I got to figure out where they're coming in.

I run over and grab my 4-quart kettle pot and put it over my head. Then I open the front door and run out. Poor Big Paul Skinny is stuck under the piano keys not knowing what to do. Well, better get a broom. I go back in, armed with my red-handled broom and start chasing the bat.

Now, the only problem with my octagon house is that it is round and I just keep running round and round trying to get that damn thing. Bats are fast and small and I can't stand them. I can handle bears, coyotes, cougars, foxes, some snakes, but bats? They all look like they've got rabies and want to suck my blood. I hate them critters. Likewise I hate mosquitoes, spiders and ticks. Living in the country they just love to get me, especially at night, sucking my blood when I can't even defend myself. I've gotten so many bites that I look like a human pincushion. Spider bites are the worst because they spit all their garbage juices inside my skin and boy do I get a reaction. That's when I want to scream. Lots of folks don't have any trouble at all with insects. But me, they love me to death.

"Big Paul Skinny, where are you going?"

"Upstairs, to get one of your white sheets."

He's running upstairs and comes out of my room waving my sheet sideways and holding it up, looking like a ghost. "You're scaring the poor little thing!"

Big Paul Skinny starts running towards me.

"You're scaring me." I run outside the front door with the little bat.

Big Paul Skinny takes off his white sheet and starts to laugh. I walk back in and take off the kettle on my head and we both have a big chuckle. It does make a difference when you've got two people working on a problem. Sometimes it can be too hard with just one, and you need help and help is miles away from you.

I like Big Paul Skinny but I know he has to go on to a bigger place. The land of sunshine will provide lots more opportunities for his life and I am on a different course. Besides, images of Ruby keep creeping up in the back of my head. I need to explore what a relationship between a man and a woman is. Not that I am all woman. Nope! I am half man and half woman. A tomboy, people might say. I am physically strong and smart like a man. I can throw a ball, run like the wind, climb trees and swing upside down. I can rough house with them, be a tough-talker, a Mr. Fix-it, and a rabble rouser. But, I need a man that can understand that part of me and not be scared by it. I need a man that can also make me feel like a woman. I'm looking for someone. Maybe Ruby will find me.

Sisterhood

A couple of months later, Big Paul Skinny has left and I am on my own working on my place. My friend, Evelyn has come a-visiting. She and I are very close. She reminds me of a princess from France. I know I've seen her face in a picture book of art somewhere.

Evelyn is a painter. There's a painting Evelyn gave me of a girl sitting in a field of dried wheat looking up at a house in the distance. Sometimes she looks like she can't walk. Her legs can't carry her. Maybe she's waiting for someone to carry her or maybe she knows someone is going to come and get her. It's got lots of possibilities and I never can settle on any one. But Miss Evelyn is here now and she's painting a wall inside my house. It's going to be Egyptian. Maybe it will have Nefertiti, an Egyptian queen with lilies. I like lilies, purple ones, or maybe irises. The painting will have lots of eyes, and beautiful women's bodies that can be seen under their sheer gowns. I'll tell you, there is nothing better than looking at women's bodies. A whole lot better then men. Women no matter what size or shape or color are so unique and pleasing. Men are okay when they look like young Apollos. That's what Ruby looks like, a young Apollo. He has long brown hair to his shoulders, and arms bulging but not too much and his chest ripples showing his strong physique.

Boy, when I think about him I get a little tingling going on. But getting back to Miss Evelyn. She reminds me of those Queens of Aragon. Her sandy blonde hair is straight and thin and flows past her shoulders. Her eyes have hardly any eyelashes. Her white skin is like porcelain. I like watching her paint. She's so quiet and dedicated. I can't wait till it's all done.

Evelyn and I like to sleep together. We always have. She's like a sister. We laugh a lot and we love to cook. We get up in the morning and make fresh raisin bread or buckwheat muffins or blueberry waffles and play Al Green on the phonograph. I love her energy. At night, we sit naked, drinking wine, and eating red spaghetti. She's my best friend and has been for a long time.

Today, she's painting and I'm working on the pump. Laddie and Sam are outside with me looking for gophers. I'm checking on some wires that have been bitten through. I've found the spot and while I'm splicing the wires I know the mailman should be coming up the bend soon. I call the dogs and decide to take a walk to my mailbox. I've got to go down through a grove of pines, maples, and wild rose bushes, past my woman-made pond and then through the barley field. I'll cross over the bridge where the beavers are working, past the pink tractor and a couple of old apple trees and head down the road to Gramer's. Around the corner from the Gramers are the boxes. Mailboxes of different sorts: painted ones, plain ones, metal ones and wooden ones. Mine's wooden. And there, underneath a rock, is a stack of letters. A letter from sister Suzanne, Hobo A-#1 and...

Hoo-whee! A special letter. This one is big. I open the envelope. It reveals a Buddy Guy record with duct tape holding the corners together. And in it, a letter written on steno paper:

*Here is a little home-town down-home low
down old time city-fried blues. Otis Spann,
Muddy Waters' (McKinley Morganfield) half-
brother, greatest of the half-brothers, greatest
of the Chicago blues and king of the
barrelhouse blues piano style. Not Bonnie
Raitt or Joni Mitchell - maybe not our blues or
your blues. Not just the blues of love that
might sweetly sadden our easy lives, but the
blues of living. I saw him before he died a few
years ago - great. My time here grows shorter
and my homesickness greater. Oh Lord have
mercy I got them easy life blues.*

Sometimes,
      Ruby Rainbow
*PS forgive a sorry scratched old favorite
record.*

I run back to the house and start to play this
Buddy Guy record. Never even heard of him. I think
it is awful special for Ruby to share his music with
me. I sit in my pink chair, close my eyes, and listen. I
day-dream about how nice it would be for me to see
him. I kind of have an ache for him in my heart.
Evelyn keeps painting but I can tell she knows how
I'm feeling. She smiles. I love that about women. The
way we communicate without saying a word. And
knowing. The women's way of knowing.

Well, I must have fallen asleep because I
awaken smelling fixings from the garden. Zucchinis,
peas, beans, eggplant, peppers, onions and broccoli
are cooking along some brown rice on the cook stove.

"Let's make a sauce, Desiree!"

"How about a peanut sauce?"

"No, how about a cheese sauce?"

"Yeah! My special mock cheese sauce."

Not made out of cow's cheese but a twist on American macaroni and cheese sauce. First, you put 1 cup of cashews in a blender, with 1 cup of water and blend it up. Then you add 3 tablespoons of sesame seeds, a jar of pimentos, 4 tablespoons of brewer's yeast, and 1/3 cup of oil that you pour in slowly at the end to thicken it up. You can add a pinch of garlic, celery seed and onion powder to spice it up, then cook it in an iron skillet until it thickens. It is the best over veggies and rice. The brewer's yeast makes it taste like cheese.

We dine at the table with lighted candles, incense and a bottle of ruby red wine. We laugh and braid each other's hair and listen to old Carole King records.

> *Winter, spring, summer or fall*
> *All you got to do is call*
> *And I'll be there...*

Evelyn is taking off today to visit her family. I'm on my own again. But another letter arrives today as well.

> *Sweet Desiree*
> *Just a quick, quickie of hello*
> *Got nothing done while my friends were here.*
> *Going to concentrate now, hopefully*
> *Was happy together -*
> *Looking forward to seeing you in a week or so*
> *Can't believe it*

Work hard play hard sleep well dream big dreams
Love Ruby

Lake Roosevelt

Today is a hot one. Too hot for me to work so I'm packing up the dogs in the truck and we're heading to Lake Roosevelt. It's not too far, there's a special spot I go to, one only the locals know about. It's an old logging road that weaves itself down to a beauty of a spot.

The Orapakin Creek flows all the way to Lake Roosevelt and is icy cold. I love to swim in this channel because it is a great swim from one side to the other side. I call the dogs in and they swim across with me. When I get to the other side I play a trick on them. I yell really loud because there is a great echo there.

Pretty soon they're barking, because they think it's other dogs and now there is a loud symphony of dogs barking. I'm sure we scare a lot of wild animals around here. Someday I'm going to have a girl and I'm going to call her Echo. Downright pretty name, I think.

The days can be long here especially when you're on your own. I am constantly playing fetch with the dogs, and watching large thunderstorm clouds move across the sky. One of my favorite past-times is playing in the clay. Bentonite clay. Very slippery. I usually take my clothes off and cover myself in the clay, head to toe. I put sticks and pieces of ferns or moss in my hair and then I call the dogs. They are quite scared of me. Keeping their distance, they cock their heads to one side, ears up and look down their long noses, trying to figure out what I am. They hear my voice but certainly I look nothing like the person they call their master. Pretty soon, I run down into the water, chasing them and oops, I hear a truck coming. Time to clean off because my skin now is feeling softer and the swollen mosquito bites are almost gone. I put on my sarong and walk up a hill so I can pick some wild flowers of yarrow, shooting stars, Shasta daisies, and buttercups for my kitchen table. Waving, I see Johnny Crush's truck. He's the beekeeper here in Fruitland hills. He's got his dog, Siskou.

Johnny is an interesting man. I met him at a gathering at the river. He has a full head of hair and a beard. A kind man with a big smiling face and a lean body with a large chest of hair. A gentle man who lives in Fruitland with his bees. You could never get me in a get-up like that strange netting over your face and those big gloves. All insects and bugs love to attack me.

I like Johnny a lot, though. I can talk to him about anything and he is so smart and good with his hands. He helps me fix my pump by the creek if I'm having trouble. I know he did live with someone a while back. The lady was kind of a drunk. At these gatherings, you'd see her pull a pint of whiskey from her back pocket and commence talking gibberish. She reminded me of my own mother.

My mother was a pretty thing. Men were attracted to her like flies to honey. My mother tried hard to be a good wife to five kids but she started partying and flirting when she was married and pretty soon she was partying and falling down drunk. She just became mean and not a pretty sight and soon my father left her. One day her liver turned yellow and she stopped breathing. I watched the whole thing. All I remember is at the very end she made a cross with her fists at me, refusing to let me get close. Ah, young women without mothers, I always say, they just keep getting stronger.

But getting back to Johnny. I like him. He has never made a move on me. We're just good friends.

"Hey Johnny! How are you doing?"

"Well hey, Desiree. What you up to?"

"Been skinny-dipping, Johnny. Got to enjoy this good weather we have here."

"Yeah, the bees are loving it. Got several boxes by Mary's place up in Colville. Would you like to go up there sometime?"

"Maybe, but this week I'm expecting someone to come visiting."

"Who's that?"

"Ah... just someone. You know you ought to check out the pow-wow sometime. Maybe you could sell your honey there, your candles. I bet you could do real well."

"Thanks, I might do that. Hey Siskou! Girl! You wanna go swimming?"

Johnny picks up a stick and throws it across the channel of the bay and Siskou dives in and Johnny follows.

"Got to go, Desiree."

He sure loves his dog, Siskou.

"Come on, girls. Let's head back to the house."

Laddie and Sam jump into the back of the truck and off we go. The truck sure runs well with its new ticker.

"Hey girls, what do you say we head over to Lake Mudgett and get some fish? Maybe we'll catch Walter."

Walter is a big old fish that swallowed my ring.

A silver ring I had designed. On the ring has an etching of a naked woman laying on her side. One day when I got out of the water and shook my body like a dog, my ring went flying up high and plunked back into Lake Mudgett. I dived back into the water and I saw a big old fish swallow my ring. I want my ring back, and every chance I go fishing I can't wait to catch that old Walter.

Lake Mudgett sits in the middle of many hay fields. Turtles rest on the old shaky pier that floats out about 15 feet into the water. I usually throw my fishing line out at sunset with some crawlers from around my place to see if I can get my evening dinner. Today the dogs wait patiently and soon something is tugging on my line. A rainbow trout. I will get you next time, Walter.

"Dogs, I've got one already. Let's head back!"

As we drive closer to the house, I see the bats are circling and catching their evening meal. I open my front door to find a beautiful bouquet of flowers in the middle of the table. This isn't a small bouquet of flowers. No, this is a very large bouquet of flowers.

"Woo, whoop, wee. Who brought this for me?"

Looking around I see no note and no one is around. No evidence in sight.

"Hmmmm," I wonder. "Well maybe the smell of fried trout will get them out of their hiding place."

I start up the cook stove, slit open the fish, and cut off the tail and head. Then I clean out its insides and roll it in some cornmeal and start the skillet sizzling with oil. Cooking fresh fish. Yummy. I walk out into the garden and pick some broccoli, spinach, and sweet Walla Wallas. I'm making some famous Greenhouse Cafe dressing of sour cream, sunflower seeds and tamari. Voila, a dinner fit for a princess. I light some candles, play Gordon Lightfoot's "Sunny Side of the Street" eat quietly as the girls chow down their dry food. Every once in a while I give them some scaly fish skin, but not too much.

"Boy, I sure would like to go riding tonight. The calendar says a full moon, girls. We'll get Sweet Chariot bridled up and get her sweating." Laddie nudges me with her nose.

The Huckleberry Mountains

Nothing is better than riding on a warm summer night in the moonlight. There's a special spring up in the valley where the water bubbles out of the ground. Soft moss surrounds it and I've got it marked with stones stacked one by one larger to small so I can see it. It's my special shrine. I place feathers from hawks or eagles there, leaves that turn green to orange, and goddess figures I make from the clay down by the river. I usually light bees-wax candles that Johnny gave me and sing or pray certain prayers to bless my days. I lay in the moonlight looking up at the stars and watch for hours, just listening to the sounds around me. It's my place to go and lay in the spring water to replenish myself. I close my eyes and dream. Dreamtime. Tonight I'll take my dogs and head up the hill and dream.

"Come here, pretty Sweet Chariot," I shake a can of oats and she comes trotting over to me, her big golden nose nudging me. "Ah Sweet Chariot, we're going out into the moonlight to get ourselves hot and sweaty. Wanna ride, little girl?"

I jump on bareback and pull the reins to the right and head up the hill to Kunter's place, past Val and Sue's cabin, then further to Steven's ranch, and up the trail to where the shrine is. Sweet Chariot knows exactly where to go and she is so sure-footed. The wind whips past my ears and whoosh, we are there, her warm body sweating against mine. She drinks from the spring as I drop to the ground. I lay out, stretched in the circle pool where I stack my rocks large to small, one by one. I light the candles, quiet my mind and dream. Dreamtime.

I awaken not too long after and dry off a bit. It's time to go back. Sweet Chariot grunts and snorts and gallops fast and swift but something starts to slow her down. Up ahead, I see it. A shadow of a man in the meadow just above my place.

"Hey girls, who's that?"

All the girls, Laddie, Sam and Sweet Chariot run faster and the dogs start barking their heads off to see who could this be. But deep down inside me I know that it has to be Ruby.

"Ruuuuby!" I yell as loud as the mountains can hear me.

To my surprise this silhouette of a man runs faster than a jackrabbit. I laugh and start kicking Sweet Chariot to catch up with this swift spirit. Just as the race draws to a close, I jump off Sweet Chariot and tackle my sweet visitor. Laughing and fighting, I wrestle him to the ground, pinning him down with his long hair covering his eyes. I blow his hair away and see those steel-blue eyes of Paul Newman.

"RUBY!" I holler like a coyote stalking her prey.

He reaches up to me and pulls me close to his body. I can't help myself. I kiss him all over, pressing my hips down against his. He holds me down tight and won't let me squirm until my breath locks into the same rhythmic beat as his.

"Aahhh!" I sigh.

Soon his hand unbuttons his jeans and I feel him enter me. It is sweet and warm and firm. I laugh and yell until all the coyotes on the hill join me. It is a full moon and what else can a girl do when the energy over powers you? He smiles not ever making a sound but moving with me as I ride him like a wild bronco. We are one and he knows it as well as I. When we are through, we pluck the wheat stalks out of our hair and walk hand in hand back up to the cabin. Silence is all around me and I hear more quiet that night than ever before. When we open the cabin's door I motion him to come up to my bed. Ruby holds me so close to him as we lay down to sleep.

I wake up with streams of sunshine coming through my windows and I look at Ruby just lying next to me. I'm hoping that he will never leave. I like looking at him. I'm noticing his forehead and nose, his chin and upper shoulders when he opens his eyes and looks at me.

"It's been awhile since we were together, but I plan to stay now. Would that be alright?"

"Sure, as long as you like." I am acting as though I couldn't do anything without him, but knowing I could.

"Want some breakfast, Ruby?"

"Yes."

Nesting

I begin my days getting up with Ruby by my side and fixing breakfast. Sort of a maternal thing, I guess. Val and Sue ride by often. They have this running joke between them to see if we have put up at least three boards of lumber on the cabin. I think they think we are making love more than working on the place. Of course they are right. We do a lot of loving and less and less work on the place as the months go by. One day, I notice things changing in my body. My tits are getting larger and hurting and also my period has stopped coming. I think as I leave to go to Spokaloo for a supply run that I'd better go over to Madison Street to see the Planned Parenthood Office.

Of course, I am pregnant. As I drive up Highway 25 from Davenport, I wonder how Ruby will take all this news. Will he stay or leave?

As I turn the corner by the white steeple church at Egypt, I notice a man walking at a brisk pace. The single long braid of black hair is a giveaway.

"Blue Heron!" I shout, honking.

I swerve over to the right and jump out. He stops and turns towards me. He smiles and opens his arms in greeting.

"Oh, how I have missed you," I say.

"Well, I knew that soon I would see you. Now that I see you, you have some news for me."

"Oh... how do you know so many things?"

"I can see it in your eyes. The eyes never lie."

"I'm pregnant."

"With Ruby's child?"

"Yes, it's true. It was a full moon when I

conceived."

"Well, it will be a strong child. But, Ruby may not accept it. In the past he has had many women."

My eyes begin to fill up with tears.

"Of course, I want the child. I am not the sort to stop this child from coming. If Ruby has to leave me, he can. In my mind, I am at peace with it."

Blue Heron places his hands on my shoulders.

"Talk to him, but at the right time. You'll know when."

I ask him to come along but he is heading in a different direction now. We part with a big hug and onward I drive the last thirty miles in deep thought. When do I tell him?

Blue Heron's thoughts kept coming back to me.

"You will know."

The Return

As I arrive up the road past the pink tractor, I see Sam and Laddie and another dog running, a white shepherd. He is a beautiful dog, very big, friendly and definitely running with my dogs. When I arrive at the cabin, I call to the white shepherd and it whips pass me and right up to Ruby.

"Well, did you bring some of your family?"

"Yes. Egypt. She's a good girl. She'll keep Laddie and Sam in line. She loves hunting and is by far the smartest of the three."

"Well, well," I say wondering if he might stay awhile longer.

We unpack the truck, unload the dog food, boards, some sheet-rock, and specialties from the co-op.

"You eat well, Desiree."

"Well, I believe in whole foods, the earth, and the healing powers of the body. What works well and what doesn't. I'm always learning new things. Working at the Greenhouse Cafe taught me a lot about whole grains, and that less meat and sugar in a person's diet is better. But now I've got to watch my own body. It needs some extra stuff."

"Why do you say that?"

"Let's go for a walk. Up the hill overlooking the valley. You round up the dogs. I'll get my stick."

I always walk with a stick. Makes me feel like I'm an explorer. Today I'm definitely exploring new territories.

The dogs take off in front of us and Ruby looks at all the plants, flowers and trees telling me what they are. He's a very knowledgeable man. He will make a good father. We walk past some shooting stars and he picks me a few and presents them with his smile.

"Ruby, I know you haven't been here very long, yet we seem to understand each other. We certainly enjoy each other's company and I love making love to you. I know most men don't like commitment and I understand that completely. But you need to know I'm pregnant. People say you might not want me to have the child. But I do want to have it. I'm just that way. Something inside tells me that this is a special child. So I'm having it. You can leave anytime you want. No strings attached."

He listens and says nothing. Then he turns around and leaves the mountaintop. Egypt doesn't go with him. I don't see him for three days.

During that time I don't let his leaving get to me. I go on with my business, mending the fence, walking the dogs, grooming Sweet Chariot and starting a patchwork quilt for my new arrival. Every night Egypt stays on the opposite hill and watches the road for any signs of Ruby. She's a true sentinel dog.

I can't be waiting. Waiting for a man is never part of the plan for me. I can only rely on myself.

After three days, I find Ruby by the creek, just squatting down, looking at the flow of the water. He doesn't look up when I walk down over the bank and through the brush. I sit quietly next to him. We are silent for a while. Then he speaks.

"Desiree, I've never wanted to have a child. Too many children in the world. But you're different. I feel different about you. I want to take one day at a time and see what will happen."

Day by Day

And that is it. I never looked at life, one day at a time. I never thought I'd live with someone. But I might as well try this. We are very alike in spirit and probably that is where we need to begin. Ruby likes to live day in and day out. We wake up every morning, spooning, together. I brush his hair. He brushes mine. We make breakfast together: bountiful granola roasted in the oven. Sometimes we ride up to Val and Sue's for milk, eggs, and cottage cheese.

We always put up at least three boards because we know we want to finish the room for the unexpected visitor. Ruby lets me sing to my records and perform, using the ladder for my stage. He helps me plant and tend the garden. He smokes pot at night and figures out the angles for the sheetrock that needs to be put up for the next day. He helps me start the truck and talks to me about what he thinks about religion, politics and love. He is very radical, though he appears to others with a soft heart. He hates racism and people being ignorant. He is well-educated and his mind is full of reasons for why so much is wrong with the world. His religion is his own. He never speaks too much about it but if someone is on the extreme right, they are 'idiots' in his mind.

I listen to different types of music with him around. Chicago blues is his favorite. Buddy Guy, John Lee Hooker, and BB King. At night, when we eat outside on the picnic table, he reads Bob Dylan lyrics to me. I've never heard much about who Bob Dylan is, but his poetry changes me. I realize my world is small and simple but his world comes from a deep need for change. Stand up for your rights! Don't be a victim! Big Brother is watching! Give peace a chance! Sometimes the turmoil of that world outside of ours is full of anger. And in time, going for long walks, working outside with the seasons, planting, tilling, picking, canning, mending, touching the soil touches Ruby's insides and change begins.

A Change

As the snow begins to pile layer upon layer and the long winter months follow, Ruby becomes restless. He is beginning to start walking around the octagon cabin etching a path. When cabin fever sets in, one needs a change. Ruby is feeling trapped.

"Desiree, I need to visit my friends in Seattle. Eric, Jenny, Joe, Darlene and Lily, Darcy, Ron Bonco, Aurora and Billy."

"Boy, you have a long list there, Buddy. It sounds like you're missing them."

"Yes, I am and there's a big party, Mardi Gras, that I want to go to. Dancing in the streets. So I'm going."

"Yep, I guess you are."

"Here's some numbers where I'll be. And by the way, we're not monogamous."

"What?"

"Monogamous."

"Magamous? Oh yes! That's what I thought you said."

What the hell is that word? Never heard of it. Couldn't even say it. Luckily I have a dictionary.

He packs up his bags and starts to leave. He tells Egypt to stay but she follows him anyway. Soon both of them are gone.

On My Own Again

I am six months pregnant. Looking now a little large and not feeling quite up to dancing even if he was going to ask me, but he didn't. The cabin is stocked full of wood, blankets, and food and it is snowing a lot. Snow is so beautiful when it begins to fall, like feathers or white orange blossoms. It just keeps falling. My heart feels heavy as I watch the snow. I have to keep busy. I pull out old clothes and start cutting swatches of velvet, lace, corduroy, and paisley. Interweaving irregular shapes with gold embroidery, I spend my time making a baby quilt. In between baking bread and stirring stews, I play my cherry upright piano lamenting my way through Gordon Lightfoot's song:

> *If you could read my mind, love.*
> *What a tale my thoughts could tell...*

In my eight-sided cabin, music soars with many hopes and fears. Pretty soon a week has gone by. No word from Ruby. I guess I am feeling a little itchy too. I've decided to put on my boots and walk down to Gramer's house. They have a phone and I'm sure they'd let me use it. It is early about 5:30 a.m. but those Gramers are up by the crack of dawn. I walk on down the road. It is a beautiful morning. The sun is shining on the crusted ice over the road. I am wearing good boots and am careful not to fall. I see Rachael and give her a wave.

"Are you okay?"

"No worries. Not due yet. Just wanted to borrow the phone."

"Sure, Desiree. Any old time."

She leads me to a room that is quiet. It is a small phone booth in her home. I pull out the paper with the numbers. I call Eric. I wake him up.

"No, Ruby's not here. He's at Darcy's."

I see her name on the paper and I call her number. She answers.

"Ruby," she whispers.

"Hello." I hear the sleep in his voice.

"Hey, it's me," I start to get an ache in my gut. "I wanted to say hi and see if you're having a good time. I am missing you."

There is a silence on the phone. My stomach is starting to feel like I'm getting morning sickness.

"I think it is best to hang up now, Ruby."

I walk home not feeling so well and go right to the dictionary. What was that word, magnongamous? I looked it up. Monogamy - the custom or condition of being married to only one person at a time. He said we're not monogamous. Hmmmm? I'm confused. We are not married. What I understand about relationships, is a person makes a commitment to one person. I thought that Ruby was making that commitment to me even though we are not married. So does Ruby want to be with other people, not just me.

I have to do some thinking about this. I am not quite sure how I feel about this idea or word. Or relationship.

Monogamy

Many weeks go by. The snow falls deeper and deeper and walking has gotten harder. I play my piano at night and sing Joni Mitchell songs. I've started to read this book called, "Open Marriage." It makes me look at my relationship with Ruby and other people's relationships. This couple who wrote it has rules. I kind of like rules. There aren't any surprises. And I figure this new relationship that Ruby and I have started needs a trial and error sort of approach. I'm not necessarily a jealous person so I do feel that maybe there is a way I can share this man with others and not let it bother me. I am willing to try and so I read and read and read. I have come to the conclusion that first I need to know if I am the primary relationship, because if I am secondary, I am outta here. And I've got my 3 rules figured out:

#1 You have to tell me prior if you're going to sleep with someone

#2 You can't sleep overnight with someone-not till the wee hours

#3 You can't do it in my bed

I have thought this out pretty carefully and when Ruby comes back we can talk about this, and Darcy.

One day, the dogs start barking and soon Mr. Ruby is opening my door with Egypt. It is awkward at first.

"Want anything to eat or drink? I'm having my afternoon tea."

He comes over to my rocking chair and puts his

head on my lap.

"I love you," he says.

Now that he says this at this time makes me feel pretty nice, but I still want to have this conversation. So I take his head into my hands and smile.

"Ruby, you know I've been thinking and reading. I want to understand you so you can understand me. So next time you don't want to be maganagamous or however you say it, this is what I want to know. Are we a primary relationship or a secondary one?"

"Primary, of course!"

"OK. Now these are my 3 rules: you gotta tell me that you're going to sleep with someone before you do it, you can't stay overnight with that person, not till 5:30 a.m., and you can't do it in my bed or our bed. OK? Does that sound fair?"

"Yes, it does Desiree. It sounds fair to me."

"OK then. That's all I've got to say."

And so it is. Ruby and I never speak about his trip or that Darcy girl. We start getting ready for Yunner Begunner. I think finding a name for "it" is the hardest thing. Rock, Wintergreen, Wind, maybe Echo. Echo is my first choice if it's a girl and Carnival would be the last name. But a boy's name is harder to find. There are Jesses, Sams, Dons, and Cliffs. But none of them seem to fit.

A Fresh Start

While I take out my Tassajara Bread Book to make fresh whole wheat bread, I look out my kitchen window and catch a glimpse of Ruby's hard brown upper body. His jeans fall just below his hip joint.

"Hmm..." I think I will join him outside in the garden.

I walk pass him with my stainless steel bowl.

"Hmm." I try to preoccupy my mind with tending to the spring garden of peas, starts of lettuce, broccoli, peppers, and tomatoes.

"It so hot. I think it's swimming time, Ruby!"

We are off to Emerson's Cove which is just between Fruitland and the Bible Camp and Lake Mudgett. There's a dirt road that winds down where the Orapakin Creek empties into the Columbia River. A beautiful inlet that has towering Ponderosa pines reflecting in its stillness. Picking wild spring shooting stars, I run down into the narrow inlet and lay my hot body in the refreshing cove. Ruby just sits on the upper bank and watches.

"Ruby, come to the shallow waters and grab some bentonite clay and smear it all over my body from head to toe. The dogs and I will dance around with twigs and feathers in our hair."

Ruby keeps staring off towards the large clouds floating in the sky.

"Attack that Ruby!" I charge with the dogs.

We pin him down and make him roll in the mud with us until he is transformed.

"The best part is to bake in the mud until it dries and cracks and then you will get a glimpse of how you will look when you are 85 years old."

After the sun sets we decide to drive back to the cabin and throw a blanket out on the grass and watch the evening stars first peek forth. The bats come out first. Then Venus. Then a million more stars and the Milky Way. We just listen and hold each other tight in the softness of the moonlit night.

The Midwife

Soon I know that my next priority is the preparation for the baby's birth. Ruby's priority is to buy himself a horse. Together we travel to Spokaloo to find his horse and a mid-wife. There is a young 4-H teenager, Sara, who is advertising a thoroughbred for sale. Ruby has looked at many horses but none have fit his criteria. They are either too small, too skinny, too dark or too light.

"Remember the horses in the storybooks? They need to have that build, and the color needs to be like the tan on my body. Also I want the horse to be quick so that my hair will blow in the wind." Ruby ponders.

We drive up to Sara's farm and Ruby's face lights up.

"See. This is a horse," he grins.

To our surprise the horse is also pregnant. Her name is Egypt, just like Ruby's dog. There is no doubt that we are to be her new owners.

In Spokaloo, I find my mid-wife. Her name is Ariel. Ariel has two children and one in the oven. I know she is the right choice for me. I sit on her woven rug breathing in and out. Her hand is steady on my belly and mine on hers. When I open up my eyes her radiant warm chipmunk cheeks calm me. Ruby sits with Ariel's old man, Don. They talk and talk, guy talk. Soon Ariel grabs Ruby's shoulder firmly and motions him to sit next to me. She places his hand on my belly and mine on his and he focuses inward. Sometimes I open up my eyes and see him intently breathing in and out. He is being drawn into the process of this new life. This is something that was hard for him in the past but now he wants to commit. As the weeks go by, we practice together the different short, panty "hee, hee, hee" and the long "who, who, who" on the exhales.

Ruby starts taking pictures of my belly and we are amazed how my body is changing. He only takes them if I am naked. He seems proud and scared at the same time. As my belly grows so does our relationship. The last two months we become closer and I notice myself slowing down. Walking has become tougher and breathing too. We gather up baby clothing from garage sales and thrift stores. Ruby spends his days, finishing building stairs from the upstairs to the downstairs. This is wonderful because using the ladder has become more difficult. Ariel reminds me that I should eat less cream and start slowing down a bit, because my blood pressure is going a bit too high. I keep thinking I am like Egypt, a racehorse. No doubt I am getting excited. This is my first time. The known and the unknown. Ariel prescribes sitting down pretty much for the remainder of my last month. I take to lounging in my sun chair and watching my garden grow while Egypt grazes on the green hay in the pasture.

The Birth

One night in a dream, I receive my instructions to begin my 'birthing' ritual. Ruby has a dream that it is a boy and that I am suppose to go to a Mexican restaurant to consume a turkey-platter plate of creamy jalapeno tostados. With a baby name book in hand, Ruby and I drive to Spokaloo to the Greenhouse Cafe. We order the tostados, while listening to Al Green playing in the background, and call Ariel about our plan of attack. She says that maybe it is best to stay in Spokaloo for the night. We call Thames and Vince, my friends from music school, and they arrange their chocolate brown music studio for our sleeping.

About midnight, my tummy begins to ripple sideways, up and down, and presto I know it is the beginning. Ariel is sent for. Carrying her big black bag filled with magical potions, we watch, wait and yawn and wait, sing, laugh, wait, wait and wait. A false alarm. But out of her big black bag comes her rare herb, black cohosh tea. It is extremely dangerous to pregnant women but if I drink just enough, it can get my contractions going. I drink 1 sip, 2 sips, and on the 3rd sip, the cup breaks, and all the hot tea spills forth upon my belly. Ariel throws me into a tub of ice-cold water, and needless to say the contractions stop.

Well with all the excitement, we realize maybe we should just relax and try to get some sleep. Thames, Ariel and Vince sleep in the living room and Ruby in the rocking chair next to me in the studio. But at 6:30 a.m., I awake with a feeling of wetness around my body, and then the pain. Yes lots of it. All I want to do is move.

"This is the real thing! No false alarm. We are beginning," bursts out Ariel.

"Whoa, if this is the beginning, then when is the end?"

To me the only course of action is to lay my full belly flat against the cool, cold tiles of the bathroom floor.

"Ah, I like this, Ariel. This will be my birthing place." as I roll from tile to tile.

"No, No, No, we must return to our new clean white sheets!"

"Ok, Ok, ok, but let's wait just a minute while this pain passes. Oh..." I moan.

"I want you to try this squatting position."

"Squatting position?" I lift my arms and try to hook my hands on top of the side of the tub. "Forget the squatting, this is my position." I rock back and forth on all fours. "Oh my God! Ariel, it's really hurting!"

"Start your breathing, whoooo, whoa, whoooooooo..."

"No Ariel, I want fast who WHOO, who!"

A sudden realization hits me. Massage is the next important key to this birthing ritual. I grab Ariel's arm.

"Ariel, I need people in here to give me a massage."

Ariel gets up and runs into the bedroom.

"Ruby, Vince, and Thames, She needs you."

"Vince, you take your hands and massage my lower back. Ruby, you take your hands here to massage my upper thighs. Thames, you take your hands and massage my feet really hard. Now Ariel, I want your hands to massage my shoulders. Now begin, all of you! Harder, harder, harder."

I exhale a big sigh of relief because it feels so good.

"Oh no...the pain again. Harder, harder, harder, faster, faster, faster."

Ruby stops massaging.

"Ruby, you can't stop."

"STOP!!!" Ariel yells.

"What do you mean stop, Ariel? I AM NOT STOPPING!"

"You have to."

"I don't have to do anything, I don't want to."

"You're in the 2nd stage, Desiree," Ariel stares me down. "Get ready to push."

"OK, OK, ok okaaaaaaaaaay, Ariel. I can't hold on much longer. I've got to do something."

"THEN DO IT! Ready, set, go!"

And so I did. I rode that glorious wave of birthing and with push 1, 2, 3. "WOOU-WOOU-WOOA!" I holler.

"It's like a purple cauliflower coming out." Ruby says in amazement.

Ruby places him into his warm, wet, bath. A smile of grand delight crosses both our faces.

"Desiree, he is so precious." Ariel places him on my stomach. Ruby and I count his toes and lay our hands upon him. Blessed be you. We shall call you Coyote.

Family

Coyote...How could he be any other name? Ruby is right. This little Coyote arrives so small, 6 lbs, 2 ounces. Maybe Ariel was wrong. I should have eaten more cream. Now this Coyote lays by my bed-side, breathing in and out making little strange sounds that wake me up. I check on him every few minutes. Ruby is exhausted from the ordeal and sleeps soundly by my side. This is the most amazing moment for me, a shift in the universe. A wanting for this, this family.

As the sun begins to break over the Huckleberry Mountains, Ruby cuts firewood, stokes the cook-stove and brings me fresh huckleberry pancakes. Attentively, he watches me breastfeed. My large football breasts amuse him. I think he wants to participate, but is afraid to ask. Doesn't every man want to suck on their mother's milk again? Our little Coyote nestles into my chest and feeds every two hours. I start making fresh bread only to be interrupted by the cries of little Coyote. Ruby makes a hanging cradle in the kitchen so I can cook and not always have to hold him. In the late afternoons, Ruby rocks him and tells him stories of the animals he has seen that day, the deer, the elk, the coyotes, and what it is like to ride on a wild horse.

We are happy, so very happy, harvesting our lush garden of greens, collecting wild roses and playing in the sun-baked truck. Ariel wants Coyote to be naked for several hours in the sunshine for jaundice. Ruby pretends to teach him how to drive and make noises of the trucks varooming down the road. The summer months pass by languidly. Coyote is gaining weight and sitting on his own. We work a little, hike a little, sun a little and party a lot with our friends. Maggie has met Johnny. Don and Jewel, Val and Sue, John and Denny and Tom and Bria have organized weekly volleyball games on the beach and barbeques at the fire-pit and swimming till sunset. Maggie starts helping Johnny at the bee farm. Don and Jewel are growing a humongous organic farm. Val and Sue provide us with eggs, milk, butter and creamy smooth cottage cheese. Yummy! Tom and Bria, well let us say they dabble in the herb "grass". In these times, the herb is definitely our choice for relaxation, not like in the 1940's and 50's where their version was alcohol. As Ruby would say, it is recreational and helps him see possibilities with life. The summer is also nurturing children. John and Denny have had Jesse, Val and Sue have had Mason, Bria and Tom have had Earth. There is a community erupting in the Huckleberry Mountains. Or rather, a brood.

Coyote

As winter sets in, the boys on the mountain grow baby fat. Except for Coyote. He has had a difficult time breathing. His nose seems to be always stuffed up. I administer warm eucalyptus packs on his chest and keep him bundled up. One night, Ruby while stroking the top of his head notices a "bulge" pushing out on top. A rather large bulge. He takes my hand in his and I stroke Coyote's soft spot. I look at Ruby and he nods. Like quick lightning, we gather our clothes and scramble down the stairs, out the door and into the truck. In no time, I am singing to Coyote in order to keep him awake.

> *"Kookaburra sits in the old gum tree*
> *Merry, merry, king of the bush is he..."*

I have no idea if he might close his eyes and never wake up. The roads are slick as can be. Ruby drives 30 miles an hour, dodging logging trucks, honking and slowing down on every hair-pin curve. All we can do together is keep steady and sing.

An hour and half later, we arrive at the hospital in Davenport, Washington. The emergency nurses bring us right in and several doctors are summoned. That's what's good about small towns. Little Coyote is put into an oxygen misting tent and we are allowed to sleep in his room and have full run of the kitchen facilities. They treat us like guests.

For the next two days, the nurses monitor his breathing, his heartbeat, and his temperature. We walk into the sterile white room and see this small child completely covered in a cloud of mist. Ruby and I hold each other tight and walk towards Coyote. Ruby sits down on one side of the bed and places his hand on Coyote's. I can see Ruby gritting his teeth as he watches him. I hold back my tears. On the third day, Doctor Evans comes in.

"Coyote might have a condition called spinal meningitis. In order for us to verify this, we need to do a test. This is a dangerous test. We will need to insert a large needle into his spine and pull out some fluid."

My eyes and mouth open wide.

"What does this all mean?" I ask, shaking my head back and forth.

"We don't know until we get the results." Doctor Evans pats me on my shoulders and off he goes.

Every mother must hate being a mother for this reason. We don't want our children to suffer. We don't want them to feel any pain. We want the pain.

"Give it to me and leave my son alone!" I scream silently.

The next day Coyote is taken from us. He disappears down a long brightly lighted corridor and through a steel door. Doctor Evans says the procedure will take a few hours. Ruby and I take each other's hands and walk outside the emergency doors to a beautiful winter's day of sunshine. Passing the cleared-off wheat fields of Davenport, we spend the next several hours in silence. By lunchtime, Ruby has wandered back into the hospital's kitchen looking over the puddings, custards and cookies. I sit with my cup of Evening in Missoula tea in the waiting room. Ruby sits down beside me with his tahini nut butter sandwich just as Doctor Evans walks in.

"Well, I have good news for both of you! Your son has no spinal meningitis. He does have a bad case of croup and the soft spot should pop back down as soon as the nasal passages are clear."

"Oh thank you, Doctor! Thank you so much!" Ruby grabs the doctor's hand.

I lean my head back on the hospital chair, close my eyes and say a little prayer. Ruby comes up behind me and begins to rub my shoulders so lovingly.

Within the next few days, the doctor's observation proves sound. The little bulge where the soft spot was pops right back down and Coyote opens his eyes. We gather our few belongings with Coyote and drive back onto the Creston-Fort Spokane road to home. Ruby nudges me to sit closer to him and I feel that we have weathered this first emergency well as a threesome.

Leaving Fruitland

In the coming winter months, there is another big decision to be made. The hospital bill has come and we do not have enough money to pay it. So we make a decision to leave the eight-sided log cabin for the emerald city of Seattle.

"We'll work for a few months to clear our debt and come back," Ruby announces. Ruby is a man of honor.

"What about your horse, Ruby?"

"Val and Sue said they will take care of her."

It has been a long time since I have had to leave my cabin for any length of time. Somehow the thought of the "big city" promises new experiences and that excites me. With a couple of army duffel bags filled, we lock up the cabin for the remainder of the winter. We carefully place on the front door a sign:

Please Respect This Home.
Good Karma will come to you.

We load up the van with the dogs and travel down the pasture, across the Orapakin Creek, past the Gramers on the right and begin our travels on the county gravel road.

Center of the Universe - Fremont

There are incredible wonders in the world and as I might have said before, they all lie between Fruitland and Seattle. There the waving wheat fields of Wilbur and Almira and rocky mesa tops towering above the healing waters of Soap Lake. The immense Columbia River cuts through all of it but disappears as the signs for Seattle start to appear.

"So, where are we going to stay when we get there?" I ask timidly.

"Darcy's."

I catch my tongue so as not to speak too hastily.

"Darcy's?" I repeat.

"She is gone for two months. We can house-sit for her." Ruby turns his head towards me for a moment.

"Good." I grin.

When our van crosses a very bright marine blue and orange bridge, I see a sign, "Welcome to the Center of the Universe." There are five or six statues of people waiting for something. Old weathered saloons and hippy hotels line the main street. Women wearing colorful skirts and lovely long haired men interweave throughout the landscape. Our car rumbles through and stops on the corner of 34th and Fremont by a sky-blue duplex nestled next to a diaper service store.

"Good omen," I chuckle.

The front unit is Darcy's. The only sign of her is

a note on the door.

> *Come on in, key is on kitchen table. Enjoy!*
> *See you in two months. Love, Darcy*

Wow! This is certainly going to be an adventure. I start to unpack, get organized and think about where to begin. Ruby has already started calling up his friends, letting everyone know that he is back in town.

"I'm working at the shipyards tomorrow," he states.

"So quick?"

"There are a bunch of us who work there off and on when we need extra money. It's just down the street."

"Should I start to look for a job, too?"

"No, just watch Coyote and we will see how we do the first couple of weeks."

I stand up in front of him and tilt my head to the left and flash an adoring smile. He grabs me tightly and leads me in to Darcy's bedroom. But I have rearranged things. I've put my own touches out. A silk embroidered shawl now is draped over our bed, twenty five scented candles of cinnamon are sweetly placed around the bed stand, and white lace covers up all of Darcy's things. It isn't Darcy's bed anymore. It is Desiree and Ruby's.

Sisterhood

The next day I get up early with Ruby, wrapping a hearty lunch up for him and then kissing him out the door. I notice another young woman across the street.

"A green farmhouse with an apple tree in front," I wonder. "I need to meet her."

After our morning meal of oats and hazelnuts, Coyote and I venture over. I knock strongly on her front door and she slowly opens it.

"Hi, I am new in the neighborhood and I was hoping..."

A cry from a baby inside resounds through the air.

"Oh, just a second," she says as she rushes towards the cry.

I slowly peek around the large wooden door to see the interior of this quaint farmhouse. Old mahogany stairs travel up from the main floor to a second story. The living room is filled with antiques of woven red oriental rugs, overstuffed purple velvet sofas and iron-wrought lamps.

Appearing from the kitchen, this barefoot, long haired hippie sister smiles.

"How old is yours?"

"Eight months." I smile proudly.

"Mine too."

We spend the remaining morning laughing, sharing secrets about ourselves and the struggles of being first time mothers. Her name is Micky. In my heart I feel she will be a true friend. Micky truly is my sister. Her warm demeanor, soft smile and attentive ears are a comfort for me.

As Ruby works into the early evening, Micky and I shop at the co-op or stroll with the boys to the Woodlawn Park Zoo and exchange herbal remedies for our sons as they fight off their first winter colds. Micky is married to Brendan. A contractor. A man's man. Ruby likes this about him. Many nights they jaunt over to the weathered saloons to play pool. Micky and I bake flaxseed cookies, stoke the fires, and drink rosehip tea. We exchange recipes for chutneys, jams and home-made breads. Our skills as healthy cooks occupy our minds until one day she hears me sing.

"Why, Desiree you have a beautiful voice. You should be out there singing."

"Really, you really think so?"

"Yes, you should be out there!"

"I sing all the time. I once met this great guy, Big Paul Skinny. He wants me to write songs with him. But he went to Los Angeles."

"Well, I bet you could meet other people here. Guitarists. Other musicians."

"You think so?"

"Yes, you've got to."

I grab her arms and swing her around. We dance a sisterhood jig.

In the next few days, we receive a Moulin Rouge postcard from Darcy.

Be home in a few days!

Her lips are imprinted on the card with a kiss. When Ruby comes home that night I show him the postcard. With a blank face, he looks up.

"Where do we go?" I ponder.

"Well...it's been two months. We have some money to pay the hospital. We can go back."

"Go back? Go back, where?"

"To Fruitland," Ruby decides.

Is that what I want to do? I hand Coyote to Ruby and walk out the front door. I walk and walk down the rainy streets to the Fremont Canal and sit on a rock watching the Nordic tugs go by, see sailboats of different grays and drenched kayakers. I have a chance to stay. Here. In a big city. I could make my talents happen. Micky says that I should sing and I believe it. There are infinite possibilities here.

As the fog horn sounds and the grey skies grow darker, I lift myself up and chant.

"I have a chance to stay." I start repeating it over and over.

When I open the door to our home, I stand squarely in its opening.

"Ruby, I have a chance to stay."

He looks up.

"Then that is what you should do!"

A Wedge

After a few drizzling mornings, Darcy arrives. The images of Ruby sleeping with her while he was in Seattle during my pregnancy stir me up inside. I am still feeling hurt by this. I keep thinking she is nothing like me. Small in stature. Short, black hair with olive skin. She looks at me. I look at her. I remind myself that she has been really generous in letting us stay here.

"Thanks for letting us stay." I say breaking the silence.

"Sure, it was no problem. You kept it looking nice."

"I've decided to stay!"

"Here in Seattle? But what about your Fruitland place?"

"We will have friends look after it."

"You know I could look after Ruby for you if you wanted to go back."

That feeling in my gut confirms that she is up to no good. I need to keep a distance from her. Don't trust her. I need to learn to trust that more now than anything.

"So... can we stay a few days until I find a place?"

"No problem. I work long hours at Harborview Hospital and I'm sure you won't be in my way."

"Yes, we will try to stay out of each other's way."

There is a low cloud that hangs over Fremont tonight. Walking from the bus stop, I accidentally walk in on Ruby and Darcy at the house. She is in the bathtub. Her small boney back faces me as I open the door. Ruby is washing her. My heart stops. I pick up Coyote and run across the slick soaked streets to Micky.

"I need to sit with you."

Micky stokes a fire in her cook stove as Sean and Coyote chase each other.

"Why don't you both stay the night?"

"Thanks." I give her a long hug.

Mothers

The next day Micky, Sean, Coyote and I walk up to the Fremont Co-op on Phinney Ridge. The Co-op building is on the corner of 39th and Phinney Ave North. It is an old 50's corner grocery store that was converted to a "Hippie Haven". Most of the food is bulk products. Large quantities of grains, rice, and dry food are in barrel containers throughout the store.

"You can work here," Micky informs me as she fills a paper bag with raisins. "You become a member, work ten hours a week for them, and get a discount on food."

"Really?" My eyes fill up with surprise.

Micky takes Coyote and Sean back to her place as I start my first job at the co-op. That afternoon amongst rows and rows of barrels, I restock steel-cut oats and brown, green and yellow lentils. I dust off shelves where exotic hazelnut butter jars stand proudly amongst the tahini and cashew butter jars of the world. In the background music of Dylan plays and the community of Phinney Ridge comes through the front doors. As I look around I see people smiling and exchanging stories about their days. This is a place to meet new people. The manager asks me to be a checker and my first customer is a blonde goldilocks woman with her young daughter.

"Here you go!" I smile. "What's your daughter's name?"

"Ally." The woman beams with pride.

"I have a son, Coyote." I pack her goodies into her cloth burlap bags.

"Oh, that's nice. My name is DeeDee Low." She lifts Ally into her baby backpack and grabs her bags.

"Are you going far?"

"No, just down the hill."

"I could help you with your bags. You're my last customer and I am walking in the same direction."

"That would be so helpful. Excuse me, but what is your name?"

"Desiree. It's nice to meet you."

As any universal mother would, I put on the backpack with Ally in it. We start to travel down the hill and to my surprise DeeDee turns to the left where the paved road switches into a gravel path. The path wanders down into a ravine past immense trees of Douglas firs and some pines where a fire engine red house emerges. Two stories. She climbs up the front stairs to the top floor.

"Does someone live below?"

"No, I am looking for someone."

"Really? Because Coyote and I are looking for a place to rent."

"Well, that sounds like an offer. Why don't Coyote and you..."

"And maybe Ruby..."

"Ruby? Why don't you come in for some tea."

On her walls hang musical instruments, foreign to my eyes. DeeDee makes us tea and we sit down in her lovely kitchen. She is musical as well as being an art historian. She has traveled to far off places like Bali, China, and South America. She loves to immerse herself in other people's cultures, their art forms, their languages and singing sounds. I see a picture of her, her daughter and a man.

"Are you married, DeeDee?"

"Yes, I am married. To Tim."

"Is Ruby your husband?"

"No, he is my old man."

"Why don't all three of you come over tonight?"

I leave her red house and peek into the lower room's windows. I begin to realize that this is going to be our next home away from Fruitland. I don't know for how long. But living below Ally and DeeDee could lead to a long continuing friendship. Running down the hills with the wind in my hair, I fling open the door of Darcy's.

"We've got a place! This great woman, DeeDee, I met her at the Co-op." I start to pack up my things.

"Wait, wait, settle down there. Stand still and tell me." Ruby gently touches my shoulders.

I stop to think for a moment about the night before. That's right. Darcy. I left.

"I'm staying here in Seattle. But I don't want Darcy to be part of us. You can stay with her. But I'm going tonight to DeeDee's with you or without you. So let's make something together or not."

Ruby slowly smiles from ear to ear and pulls some vegetables from the bin.

"You really do want to stay?"

"Yes, yes I do."

That night at the fire engine red house of DeeDee's, Ruby knocks on the door. When Tim opens the door to meet us, Tim catches Ruby's eyes. They both start laughing. Tim is an old friend of Ruby's. He met Ruby at the Red Square on the University of Washington campus.

"It was a free showing of the film, *The Harder They Come*. I was so excited about the soundtrack. I started yelling at anyone who looked like me. Ruby looked like a likely suspect so I went over to him and said, 'you've got to see this. A free showing, man. It's about this Jamaican, a rural boy who comes to the big city to become a singer.'"

As Tim starts singing, Ruby joins in.

> *The harder they come,*
> *the harder they fall, one and all.*

DeeDee brings me into her cozy kitchen. There are cupboards and cupboards bursting with color: canned golden peaches, red peppery chutneys and forest green pickles.

"Funny how small the world is." DeeDee opens up a bottle of red wine.

"It seems everyone is open to new friendships here."

"Cheers to that!" we all raise our glasses and begin to talk the night away.

Our Home

That week we move in. I start to paint the walls orange and red against the brown-framed doors and windows. There is a wood-stove, a small bedroom for us and an even smaller bedroom for Coyote. First on my list is to find a piano. I need one if I am going to start singing more. I search the Phinney Ridge Paper and find an old spinet. A Baldwin made just the right size: small. It is going to fit perfectly in the living room, but how are we going to get it down to our new place? Ruby and Tim have come up with this crazy ass idea. They are going to tie the piano on to the back of Tim's truck and since the piano is already on wheels, just roll the truck slowly down the hill with the piano behind it. When you're poor, you do these crazy ass things.

On Saturday, the piano comes rolling on down to the bottom of the hill and then up a little hill before we can even reach the stairs going down to the new place. Tim has called Eric, Jude, and Peter from Corn House to help. Corn House is a community of artists living in a big yellow house near the Buckaroo Tavern in Fremont. They tie the piano up with large ropes and create a pulley by wrapping the ropes around a tree. Heave Ho! Heave Ho! HEAVE HO! UP THE HILL WE GO! HEAVE HO, HEAVE HO, DOWN TO THE FRONT DOOR! There the little spinet slides into a corner of the living room cuddling close to the wood stove.

Friends

Invitations! Invitations! A letter is always welcomed. This one is from the boys at Corn House. An invitation to a party, a special party. Meeting new friends, Ruby's friends. I am a little nervous. Always being on the other side. The newcomer. The new friend.

I'm walking down to Fremont to see what "Deluxe Junk" has in its bargain chest. Always and without fail, I can find a treasure. All the clothes are hung on the walls from the top of the ceiling to the bottom of the floors. Vintage hats, shoes, aprons, lingerie, suits, jackets and dresses. I see a dress. The one that I think will razzle-dazzle any onlookers. It's a 1940's vintage dress made of see-through black crepe with small bouquets of pink flowers appropriately placed, revealing just enough of my breasts. It also has diamond studded buttons. I feel very French in it. Wearing a black beret to accent it, I feel *tres chic*. I am buying it.

Friday night arrives and I ask Micky to babysit. At the yellowy Corn House, people are pouring in the main door, side doors and back door. There must be 200 people at this party. Ruby quickly disappears. Someone sees me.

"You have the most amazing smile," he says.

"Why, thank you. I don't know anyone here."

"Well, come with me. I'm Marty. I'll show you around."

Marty has a nice face. A round face with warm eyes and a round belly to match. He dances with me and introduces me to everyone.

"Everyone! Everyone welcome!" Marty clamors. "This is Desiree. She's new to Seattle."

My smile grows larger and my confidence swells. I strut through a door that leads into a darker room with a maroon velvet couch in the middle of it. Eight beautiful women are draping themselves around a man. One woman has her legs draped over his. One woman is touching his hair and shoulder and another one is standing behind him whispering in his ear. I don't recognize that the man is Ruby at first. I think I have entered a forbidden room. But then I catch his steel-blue eyes looking at me. The women don't change their positions when they see Ruby's eyes meeting mine. They just go about their business of whispering, touching, leaning, laughing as I enter their private room. I smile at Ruby in a rather smirky way.

What pleasures Ruby seeks. Always women. Many women. Is it becoming clearer that I am one of many? I decide to look at each of these seductresses. Not to say anything but just to stare. After a minute or two, I walk forward with a clear intention. I am the primary lover of Ruby and none of you have that. Slowly I lean into Ruby's face and kiss him very hard, long and deep. I think I've made it clear who I am. Yummm!

Strutting out into another room, I meet Jude, Darlene, Eric, Aurora, Cody, Peter, Mary, Ron, Stephen and many more. I dance all night long, drink champagne, and giggle and giggle and giggle.

Men

When I put Coyote to sleep I think of his funny behavior. He has a bed that we built out of plywood and two-by-fours. We put him in the bed at night, but he won't sleep on it. He sleeps on the floor. We've put padding on his bed, but I always find him on the floor in the morning. It's curious. He also does this adorable routine of taking his favorite Superman shirt and his faded blue jeans and laying them out on the floor before he goes to sleep. First the shirt, then his underpants, then his jeans, then his socks and then his shoes. They are all laid out in order as if someone was wearing them but the person isn't actually in them. Coyote is prepared, just like a fireman, at all times in case of an emergency. There's a knock on my door.

"Hm?" I'm not expecting anyone.

I stop washing the dishes and look through the peep hole. I'm surprised.

"Jude." I remember that he was at the party as I open the door.

"Thought I'd come by to see what you were up to."

"What a surprise."

"Want to go for a walk?" He leans in a little closer to me.

"Sure, I'd love to, but Coyote is sleeping," I wipe my hands on my apron. "Sit down if you have a moment."

He eyes a place to sit. I notice he takes the comfortable couch.

"Want some tea?"

"Sure." He flashes a Cheshire smile.

I sense that he is up to something. It's rather amazing and flattering to have a man visit me. I'm curious. He is attractive. He totally digs me. So I return with two cups of "Evening in Missoula."

"So... Jude, what are you doing today?"

"Not much, just thought I'd see what you were doing. You remember the other night?"

My eyes open wide. Hm, the other night? I was having so much fun, dancing, giggling and drinking. Oh, I hope I didn't do anything misleading.

"I was just having so much fun."

Jude leans in a little closer.

"A little fun? I think you wanted to have a little more fun."

"Jude, I am flattered." My cheeks become a shade redder. "But this isn't a good time." I lean way back into the couch.

He presses forward and is on top of me quicker than a snare catching a possum.

"Wow, you're a great kisser but you have to go now..." I see Coyote's door starting to open. "Coyote, you're up!"

I jump up. I'm on my feet and rush to Coyote's bedroom door which thank God is just six feet away. The tired little soul walks out with his blanket.

"I think it is best for you to go." I whisper to Jude.

He gives Coyote a tickle and prances out the door. Morning surprises like this will keep me smiling for the rest of my day. There's a knock on my door.

"Oh, another admirer?" I chuckle when I see little Ally opening the door.

"Let's go play!"

"Certainly, we say."

My Audition

It's a beautiful day. The sun has parted the clouds a little and it is an afternoon planned for "make-up faces." Coyote and I pull out my old boxes of white make-up, comical hats, and oversized coats. We invite DeeDee and Ally to play with us. As we all help each other, our faces take the shape of clowns.

"Desiree, I heard you singing the other day. You have a beautiful voice."

"Thanks, DeeDee."

DeeDee snaps a photo of us as we dance like characters in a Tom Wait's circus sideshow. Enjoying each other as mothers and friends, I feel that this is a natural and pleasant place to be. Yet part of me struggles with wanting time to explore myself.

"DeeDee, I would like to figure out what to do with my voice while I am here."

"Well, I heard from a friend of mine that there is an audition tomorrow."

"Should I go? Should I try?"

"Yes!" Everyone applauds. "You must go!"

"Can you watch Coyote?"

"No problem. Go, Desiree. You've got to try."

The next day, I do. I prepare some music. I put on my purple jumpsuit that fits me well. With a hope and a prayer, I find myself with several others waiting for a chance to audition at A Contemporary Theatre. Stan Kerr sits patiently while I burst out with my song, "Maybe This Time."

"Desiree," he says, "you have a beautiful voice, but there's something missing. I can see that you move well. You need to take acting lessons, then your package could be a killer."

"Acting? Okay. I'll take acting."

I walk out not feeling defeated but knowing that there is more I need to know. Acting.

"Stan Kerr says I need acting classes. He says there's a woman, Christy Saylor, who teaches acting classes at Highland Community College. She's really good."

DeeDee keeps nodding her head up and down as I ramble about how my audition went.

"Well, sign up for the class now."

I do. I look in the telephone pages and call the administrator and they say they'll send me a catalogue. I can start right away. Highline is definitely a bit of a jaunt, about forty miles away from Fremont, the center of the universe, but I am determined and I have a Dodge Dart.

I will announce it at dinner. Ruby obviously is not in a good mood. There is something brewing inside of him.

"Ruby, I auditioned today. Stan Kerr said he loved my voice but he said I'm in need of acting lessons." I tell him as I prepare plates of spaghetti with red sauce.

There is complete silence.

"Good for you, mom."

Ruby shovels spaghetti into his mouth.

"What's up, Ruby?" I gently inquire.

"I'm going to do another job. The shipyards are laying me off and in order for us to make it, I'm going to start being an assistant to a surveyor. Maybe I'll become a surveyor. Down in Kent."

"Kent? Where's that?"

"About thirty-five miles down south, past the airport. A long commute."

"Is Highline Community College down there?"

"Yes."

"Well, I could go to the community college down there. I could teach singing. That would bring in some extra income." I hope that Ruby will agree with this plan so that the acting will work too.

"What about Coyote?"

"Well...I'll find a place for him. A good place. It's a good time for him to be more social. Ally and him..." but I can sense Ruby is tired.

He just wants to eat in peace. We all eat quietly as I devised a plan.

Raising Coyote

Ruby makes me mad today. He is constantly saying that I'm a marshmallow. A marshmallow. Apparently the way I'm raising Coyote is like a marshmallow. Well, I think Ruby's a taskmaster. Where do we get the tools or knowledge to raise a kid? I think that I know how to do this job. How can he tell me what to do? I raised four children including myself in spite of a volatile alcoholic mother. Ruby only raised himself. Walking by himself all over the streets of Chicago, he would hold on to the pockets of strangers so he could play at the amusement parks or museums.

Today I've decided to take some action. A Montessori School called The Learning Tree is advertising on some telephone poles. "How to Talk So Kids Will Listen and Listen So Kids Will Talk." I'm going to have both of us go to "Parenting School." I march right over to the Montessori school on 15th Street.

"I want to be in your parenting class."

"Great. No problem. It's Monday nights at 6:30 and child care is provided."

"I want to buy two copies of the book."

I've need to get a head start on Ruby. Ruby is a fast reader. I'm excited. I like to learn new things and probably this will help Ruby and I communicate better. This will be a real challenge for me because I am not much of a reader. But I am determined. I pull out my old dictionary just in case and study the word, "marshmallow." Soft and gives. Opposite of strong and consistent. A confection of sweetened paste. Marsh. A low lying wet land, swamp or bog.

The parenting book is about 232 pages.

"You'll like this book. It's going to be very helpful. You won't give in to Coyote's wants. You won't do things for him," Ruby declares as he finishes the last page of the book.

Of course I'm still reading the book. I look up from the book dumbfounded.

The woman standing in front of us explains that we will form two groups to discuss the book. I am very happy that I will not be in the same group as Ruby's.

She explains very slowly and carefully, "If the child's disposition would be tired or hungry..." I look over and see Ruby is talking up a storm in his group. I listen to what people are saying in my group. I've read the chapter and want to talk about a situation with Coyote that occurred this week. I raise my hand.

"I never lose my cool with Coyote. It seems like I have a sixth sense of what he is doing. We have a great time together. He is a wonderful child. Ruby says I give into everything. He says I am not in charge. I am not consistent. But Coyote never gives me any problems."

"Has anyone ever had a child say that he is tired?"

Another parent raises his hand.

"My child is tired even after he has taken a nap."

Another parent explains that sometimes she feels so bad when her child is so sleepy and she is trying to get her child ready for school but he just won't get dressed.

"As parents you should let your children trust

their own perceptions," the woman explains.

I am thinking about this statement hard. I am thinking how these situations lead into arguments between Ruby and me. I raise my hand again.

"Coyote sometimes gets tired when we go on a big hike. He can't walk very long so he wants me to carry him. It's a long hike into the forest. We've been hiking maybe one mile or so and Coyote looks like he is dragging. So... I pick him up and put him on my hip. Ruby hates this. I can see that he is pissed. I explain to Ruby that he is just too tired. Am I a marshmallow?

The woman looks perplexed.

"Desiree, let's do some role playing. Chrissy, you play Coyote."

Chrissy chimes in quickly.

"Ma...I am too tired. Pick me up!"

"Now before you pick him up, Desiree, what could you say to Coyote?"

"Well, I could get down to his level and say, 'Oh, let's just take a break right now and maybe get some fuel in us.'" Then I would give him a power bar.

"That's good. Taking some time to assess the situation is good. Then what would you do?"

"Hm. I'd say to him, 'Coyote do you think you could walk now a bit more so we can head back to the car.'"

"Yes, and that would be a great way of getting him to rest a little, eat a little and check if he could walk a little more."

"But what if he couldn't do it anymore?"

"Well, then you would have to pick him up."

I sit there for just a moment. Yes. Maybe I need to add that extra step. That makes sense.

Strong Choices

My first acting class at Highline is large. About thirty five people. Christy Saylor is very slender, a woman about forty years old with curly blonde locks. She reminds me of a Jessica Lange type. She is wearing a white pullover sweater over white jeans with white knitted leg warmers. I am thinking that she was probably a professional dancer in her time. She seems smart, witty and funny.

"When you audition, you must have a monologue."

She explains that it is a dialogue with you and someone else, only the other person isn't there with you. So you have to imagine they are. I have done some acting in high school so I've decided I will do Billie from *Born Yesterday*. Everyone sits down as the theater becomes pitch black except for the light on the stage for us.

I enter from one side of the stage and position my chair. I am a little scared, but I take the stage and speak from my heart. I love this moment. I love that Billie isn't too smart. She has never read a book and she wants to learn, just as I do. She wants to be smart.

"Desiree, that was good. I want you to start working on the New York accent. You can start auditioning outside the class."

In the coming weeks, Christy has each actor enter the a fully-designed kitchen on stage. We are to enter as an animal. No talking. Wearing my apron, I start to make a pie as a bird. My long beak moving and shifting back and forth. Shifting my head to the side so that I can look through my bird eyes to see what I am doing. My hands now are wing extensions. Coyote and I have been watching animal shows so I can practice. Both of us imitate animal's voices and movements.

"Ma, you make a good bird." Coyote is so joyous and loves to fantasize just like his mom.

Christy informs me that I will be playing Miss Polly Brown in "The Boyfriend." Terry Patton is going to play opposite me. He is tall, slender, and very good looking. Each rehearsal we tap dance and sing as clowns playing Pierre and Pierrette. The lost lovers. Of course I am falling secretly in love with Terry on stage. During breaks, we take long walks on campus and tease each other in the bushes. He has an apartment in Seattle and so one night I meet him there. Ruby finds the cast list phone numbers and calls me at Terry's apartment. Even though I have told Ruby that I am going to meet Terry, Ruby is extremely angry.

"I want you to come home now."

I stop making love to Terry and run home to a phone smashed against a broken window.

Ruby sits there silent. He is injured by this man.

"Ruby, you said you wanted our relationship to be non-magnagamous. Remember how it was with Darcy? I am trying to understand what you want. I am trying to follow the rules. Remember? You said that emotions weren't going to get involved in this."

Search and Rescue

Ruby has been cocooning himself away from me for a week now. Search and rescue. I don't even know where to look for help but I find S.I.S.T.E.R.S. (Seattle Institute for Sex Therapy Education and Research) in the telephone book. Kay Larson, the rescuer is a behavior modification expert. She is tall, slender, has a PhD and is masculine. She appears rigid and intellectual but obviously has her sexual side working for her. She runs her classes in this old ma and pa neighborhood storefront by the Honey Bear Bakery. The classes that are offered there are everything from anal stimulation to reaching an orgasm to stripping yourself of your sexual hang-ups. It all seems underground and very hushed up. If you would ask the average person on the streets of Seattle about it, they would have never heard of this organization. It is on the fringe. Perfect for us.

Kay has us sitting down in an eight-by-ten foot room in two old grandma Goodwill easy chairs. Kay is not a tidy woman. Stacks and stacks of manila files hang on for dear life on her hand-hung shelves. She has many degrees on the wall, M.S., D.H.S., LMHC, and FAACS.

"Always pay cash," Kay says "and if you need a receipt, don't bother. Why are you here?"

"Ruby, my partner, wants to have relationships with other people. But when I do it, he becomes angry and upset."

Kay looks hard at Ruby.

"Do you want this relationship to work?"

Ruby lowers his eyes. "More than anything."

Kay looks at me.

"Do you want this to work, Desiree?"

"Yes, I do! Ruby is my soul mate. We have a son. But Ruby gets quiet. Sometimes he's quiet for three days."

"Are you willing to talk to Desiree now? Ruby, can you tell her how you feel?"

Ruby moves back and forth in the grandma easy chair trying to get comfortable. "I don't know what I feel."

Kay looks at both of us.

"Men are meant to wander. It's the history of sexuality. Desiree is trying to understand this. Both of you have given each other rules. Rules are fine, but emotions come into play-and they will be there. They will be a present for you to deal with. Anger and revenge. Respect them. They will test this path that both of you are attempting to travel. You will need to continuously talk about this."

The Test

The next things that people do when they are working things out is to keep testing. Pretty soon Terry, Ruby and I are partying together. At these parties we experiment with coke while we dance and drink. We are actually enjoying each other's company. I think Ruby is trying the "let's be friends" approach. If we are all friends, then maybe it will be easier.

One day in class Christy approaches me.

"I want you to do this scene from *Otherwise Engaged* by Simon Gray." She hands me the play. "It is the scene where you bare your breasts."

My lips form a perfect O. "Oh, do I have a say in this?"

"No," she politely responds back.

I keep reading the scene over and over and I keep repeating the same question: Can I do this in front of an audience? Friends, yes, or the forest friends, yes. Lovers yes or in the fields of Fruitland, yes, but in front of my acting peers? It feels different to me. A question mark with a capital Q. I am bound and determined to prove myself to Christy. Thank God Terry isn't going to be my scene partner. That is a big plus. Graig, a closeted homosexual, will be. I guess that will be okay. Graig is very sweet and a nurturing kind of guy. We spend hours on the big stage practicing, practicing, and practicing. Not only do I have to bare my breasts but I have to do an English accent on top of it.

When I get to the part where I have to take off

my shirt, I take it off but I leave my bra on. Graig thinks it's cool and doesn't even make a big deal of it. I tell him that when I was young I used to stand up and look down at my feet but I couldn't see my feet because my breasts were too big. After Graig and I have done the scene so many times, we think it will be okay to leave the bra off.

"Desiree, you certainly have big breasts."

"Told you." We both laugh.

It is the day of the presentation of our scene. Graig and I are backstage holding each other and pumping each other up. We can hear all the people filing in. Suddenly, no sound. Then, "Places!"

Graig grabs my hand and we enter the back of the stage in the dark and take our positions. The lights come up. And Simon and Davina take the stage where Graig and I once were.

> Simon: I'll get you something to wipe your shirt."
> Davina: Don't bother, it's far too wet. But another drink, please.
> Simon: Of course.

Simon takes my glass and walks to the drink table. I feel my shirt is wet and pull it off and put it on the chair. I pick up my purse and cross over to the fireplace and take out my handkerchief and proceed to dry my neck and chest while looking at a fake mirror on stage. Simon turns and falters slightly and then brings the drink over to me. I turn to Simon and then we go on with the scene as normal just like how we have practiced it. Like brushing your teeth on stage. The last phrase, the last moment, the last breath, and the last final light cue.

Darkness falls, and then Graig and I walk off the stage. He guides me as I grab my shirt. We stop and hug each other tightly.

"We rocked!"

This event was huge for me. Christy gathers everyone in the class to talk about the scene.

"Desiree and Graig did a brave scene today!" Everyone applauds us. "Desiree, the only thing I noticed was that when your shirt came off, your voice became a little softer when you spoke."

I nod my head realizing that I didn't even notice that it did go quieter. I am amazed that I even did it. Certainly, I will keep working on my voice so I can project even when my breasts upstage me.

Universal Mothers

Coyote is falling in love with people. Everywhere we go, all the old people become his grandmas and grandpas. We meet Mary just down the street who has a day care and she is willing to take Coyote during the day while I take classes at Highline. She is a universal mother type. Children love running around her house, just being kids, doing lots of art projects or playing in the back yard on riding toys and slides. Coyote is so social there.

"Coyote, do you want to go here while I am at school?"

"Yes I do, Mom!"

"Mary, I could help you part time and teach the kids how to sing."

"Kookaburra sits in the old gum tree..." Coyote begins to sing with me as though we are two old time vaudevillians auditioning for a job.

"Great. I have a piano and material from fabric stores and we can set up a curtain for story time."

"I've got oversized shoes and hats from the Goodwill. Also some full-sized masks and half-sized ones too."

"Great! And I have lace and capes."

It is one big house of stuff. Everything is in-limits, not off-limits. I get the kids to learn acting exercises by being animals. We walk and talk, roar and squawk. It is our daily ritual.

Now that Coyote is on his own and loving it at Mary's, I've decided to start teaching singing lessons down at Highline. It couldn't be more perfect. I contact the music department and Christy gives me a great recommendation. I can use a room during the day when I am not taking a class and teach a few lessons a day. Terry wants to take lessons from me and so do Graig and Sherri. Coyote and I make this fantastic, colorful flyer and I put it up on the bulletin board right by the theatre. Lots of people who come to our shows should see it. I've already gotten a phone call from a girl named Robin who sings in a cover band and a sweet young man named Ira Melody. This is what I want to be able to do, pay my way while I am studying. Plus it will keep my voice in shape for the upcoming spring musical.

The Boyfriend

In *The Boyfriend*, my favorite scene begins with a violin cadenza. It's slow approach introduces "Poor Little Pierrette." Me. During the rehearsal, the lights on the stage are immensely hot. My white make-up feels unusually wet: wetter this evening than last night. I look up stage right at the spot-light that illuminates the moon. I stand there, looking up in my white satin clown outfit waiting as Tony, played by Terry, approaches. My body stands rigid as my right arm lifts slowly towards the moon. I glance quickly and see that Terry's white make-up has large drops of sweat beginning to bead upon the surface of his skin. He raises his left arm which moves his upper body and face about one foot from mine. My left foot is starting to twitch. Oh my God, I hope the audience can't see this. I beam towards that moon again.

Damn, I forgot to gargle before this act. What am I thinking about? The most climatic part of the scene and I have bad breath. Will Terry ever forgive me?

Terry's eyes meet mine. He begins to move towards my face. One, two, three, the violin solo begins and my eyes leave the moon and travel towards his eyes.

"Oh Tony, I am such a sad clown, please kiss me."

My mouth naturally curls upwards as I cock my head to the left looking demure. I am thankful at this moment because my arm which has been extended for the last thirty measures of music can come down now and position itself to a clasping position with my other hand. My left foot is still twitching. Now, my thigh is too. God, I hate when this happens.

My mantra is just keep breathing into your thigh, your left foot, keep smiling, and act demure at Terry. Terry doesn't look so good. His eyes are kind of glazed over as if he is not in the moment. You've got to be in the moment.

Christy Saylor has said this over and over again. I know she is going to give us director notes on this very thing. I wonder if I should make cross-eyes now or something? Would that help make Terry be more present? Certainly the audience wouldn't see it. It would be for only a second. Could I dare? Nope, can't do it. He is closing his eyes. The conductor's arms are getting really big now on the downbeats on the song. I love this part; how the bass, violins and cello crescendo back and forth in the minors key before reaching the major one. Terry never sees the orchestra. But I have a bird's eye view of Maestro Thulean as he swirls his baton upward and downward in this glorious section of the "Poor Little Pierrette."

Terry's mouth is about one inch from mine. He has to kiss me. For my lips are like every young virgin's waiting in my virgin state of excitement for that kiss, that first kiss, which I have hoped for for the last two hours of this musical.

Now I slowly close my eyelids, my mouth puckers forward, my upper body leans into his as the conductor retards the orchestra's last chord. His red lips meet my red lips right on cue. I hear that inevitable sigh of many of the female audience members. And that is it, the musical.

The Picnic

It's been raining like cats and dogs. I keep wondering why the phrase cats and dogs exists. So I look it up like everything in an old sayings book.

> *They say that there never has been reported weather conditions involving cats and dogs but apparently there has been reports of small creatures like frogs and fishes scooped up by strange weather conditions.*

I like to go deeper into myths because my heritage is of the Emerald Isle.

> *Dogs and wolves were attendants to Odin, the god of storms and sailors which are associated with rain. Witches who often took the form of cats suppose to have ridden the wind.*

As Coyote and I look out against the rain pelting the windows and the fast-moving billowy clouds racing by, we decide to go on a picnic.

"What do you say to a picnic with all the trimmings, like fried chicken done my way, fried in olive oil with a light dusting of potato flour, and potato salad, with onions, celery, potatoes, mayo, and rice vinegar, and also my favorite cole-slaw with chopped apples, carrots and raisins. What do you think?"

Coyote and I search in our layaway duffel bags for our bright bumble-bee-yellow rain pants and jackets. We find tucked away our bright yellow rain hats to match. We start to dance around while I put on the Beatles, "Yellow Submarine."

We all live in a yellow submarine,
a yellow submarine...

Ruby finally arrives home from work. With a picnic basket full of goodies and Ruby in his very own bright yellow fashionable rain gear, we venture to Lincoln Park.

Lincoln Park is a 135-acre park in West Seattle. The Duwamish tribe called it "Tight Bluff" because of the immense growth of towering trees. You can swim in a heated salt-water swimming pool but only in the summer. Instead we go to Williams Point and look out as the Fauntleroy-Vashon Ferry pummels the crashing waves of the Puget sound. In the park are swing sets and picnic shelters. Ruby, Coyote and I swing to try to touch the trees with our toes.

"I'm hungry, Ma."

Why certainly, our picnic! We jump off the swings to splash in all the puddles with our rain boots.

"Run to the picnic shelter!" Ruby joins in the fun.

Opening up our wooden basket, I place a warm covered container of chicken on a yellow gingham table-cloth just right for three. Ruby pours sweet hot hibiscus tea into our yellow mugs. We look out at the gray clouds signaling another unleashing of cats and dogs as we giggle.

"We defy the rains, we are having a summer delight!"

Coyote points his greasy fingers to the clouds above.

"Fried chicken, potato salad, and cole-slaw!" we all chime in.

My Birthday Wish

It's my birthday and Tim, DeeDee, Jude, Eric and Cody are throwing a party at Corn House for me. Marty will be there and Micky, my first friend from across the way of Darcy's old house. Lily from Community Produce with semi-truck driver Arlene, librarian Aurora, Billy the poet, Ron Bongo and Don Liddel the ham radio operator are also on the list. The Pot Belly Boys and their friends will be there. Brendan, Micky's ex who now is playing poker with Ruby, is coming as well. Of course at Corn House parties, everyone shows up. The house is packed with two hundred folks. The Pot Belly Boys are getting it down with their old favorites and people are dancing, smoking, and consuming kegs in the back. There's lots of movement and commotion. I love parties. I like the fact that I walk in and everyone is so welcoming and flirtatious and having fun. I just feel I'm me. Me, on my own.

I wave to Marty who hugs me to his big barrel chest. We dance a little, smoke a little, and then I do-si-do to another partner like in contra dancing.

I wave to Micky in the kitchen. She signals to me and I hurry over to the kitchen.

"I have a surprise for you. Happy Birthday!" She presents a giant carob cake with thick carob honey icing.

"You shouldn't have."

"Well of course I should have. It's the best day of your life." Her sweet Croatian eyes connect closely with mine as if there is something hiding deep inside them. She puts the cake down.

"Micky, come with me, let's dance." I take her hand, making no effort to wait for her response, and we both run into the dining room. Eric, the sax man, has just taken over the helm of the band and the party is grooving to a Rolling Stones Song, "You Can't Always Get What You Want."

I am singing the words loudly over and over. Micky joins in. Soon everyone is pumping up and down, over and around. Micky closes her eyes and relaxes as we dance together. I love dancing with women. We always have fun laughing, exchanging moves, copying each other, and trying to keep our bond going. The tune is over and we hug each other for a long time.

"Happy beautiful day to you, sister," Micky pulls away. "I've got to talk to you."

"Sure." But then Jude slithers up behind me as the next tune starts and whispers in my ear.

"You drive me wild, Desiree."

"Ah Jude." I turn around as Micky retreats back to the kitchen.

"I heard your play is going great."

"Yes, the musical. Yes, come see it." I yell over another great tune, "I Can't Get No Satisfaction."

The living room is packed with sweating bodies and sloppy drinking.

"It's heaven to be this free," I yell.

"Darcy came with me."

"Darcy?" I started to say and then realize she is behind Jude.

"Hey, Darcy."

"Hey, Desiree."

"You're back."

"Yes, and Jude boy is keeping me true."

I glance at Jude.

"Wow, Jude. Congrats for you."

"Are you and Ruby still hanging?" Darcy senses my energy towards Jude.

"Of course," I smirk. "Why?"

"We heard that Micky and him are having a thing."

I feel an arrow being shot into my heart. My knees are starting to shake but I quickly reinforce them.

"Oh, you know Ruby. Maybe magnanimous was never his thing."

Suddenly the coal black-haired Darcy turns and spoons Jude's backside into hers. I march back into the kitchen.

"Micky, is it true?" I ask. Micky stops chewing on the sweet piece of cake she has baked.

"Desiree, I was going to tell you. I just thought he told you."

"Nope. he has a habit of not keeping the rules."

"Oh, I'm so so sorry."

"Yeah... well, happy surprise to me."

The mood on the dance floor changes as Eric, the sax man directs everyone to sing,

"Happy Birthday to you, Happy Birthday dear Desiree..."

DeeDee comes rushing in and scoops up the cake with candles blazing and Micky joins the crowd as I watch the flickers of the candles and try to make a wish.

Wishes Do Come True

That wishful event brings me closer to what I want. I win a scholarship for continuing with Christy and a chance to try out for the Professional Training Program in Seattle. It seems that my life is changing with greater directions, not just being a mother to my son or just a lover to Ruby. I kept thinking that there are greater things for me if I just put myself out there.

Christy has prepared me with valuable skills in play after play and scene after scene that we have performed. Announcements for scholarship money and audition dates are laid down before us. It is narrowed down to five women for the entry to the University of Washington's Professional Acting Program.

The morning of the final auditions, Coyote has become extremely sick. Ruby confronts me.

"You should choose between Coyote and this audition."

"No, I'm sorry. You are here too. You stay; I need to go. I need this for me!" I run out of the door leaving my son with his father to take care of him.

"I need this for myself," I keep repeating like a mantra. "Coyote will survive and so will Ruby."

I will become stronger by this situation of raising a child and trying to raise myself up in the bigger picture of our separate worlds.

The letter came in the mail today. I was afraid to open it. It is an official envelope with typing in the upper left hand corner:

Professional Actors Training Program

University of Washington

Tearing one side and gingerly sliding the letter out, I read the sad news.

> *Thank you for auditioning for the Professional Actors Training Program. You were one of five finalists but we have decided that we cannot offer you a position in the program.*

My heart sinks a little bit lower in my chest. Coyote sees my discomfort and walks up to my leg and grabs my pants.

"Ma, what's wrong?"

"Oh, just a bump in the road," I pick him up and give him a big old hug.

"Can we fix it?"

"We can fix anything. We just have to be creative."

"Let's make something, Ma!"

Smiling and holding Coyote, I sit down with him next to his favorite blocks to build a multi-dimensional structure. Triangles, cylinders, and square blocks hide our imaginary friends and foes. In this state of playing as children, I come up with plan B. You always need a plan B in life.

"Let's go for a ride, Coyote. To Volunteer Park."

"Yea, Ma!"

We gather up snacks, water, my letters of recommendations and my resume. Driving across the Fremont Bridge, along Lake Union, and the back street up Mercer sends you to Harvard Ave to where prestigious artists such as Isadora Duncan and John Cage have strolled while attending Cornish College of the Arts. With Coyote on my hip, I walk in to the administration office.

"Can I still apply to the Professional Actors Training Program here?"

"Why yes." A friendly smile greets Coyote and me across the room.

"Here are my resume and the letters of recommendations."

"These are the remaining dates to audition."

"Great. I will take this Saturday at 10:00 a.m."

"Wonderful. Fill out these forms...and what a cute boy you have! What your name?"

"Coyote." He proudly flashes his beautiful smile.

"What a sweet boy you have."

"Ma you said we are going to Volunteer Park."

"Yes I did, and here you go and thank you. I will see you on Saturday."

The beauty of this old stucco art deco building and the grand dark wood hallways gives me a sense that there are yet other possibilities and plan Bs. You may not always get your first choice in life. But second choices are second chances in educating yourself.

A Chance

The day of the audition feels right. Everything about it is right. The long corridor, the small room with three people sitting at a long grand table. The silence before. The silence afterwards. What are they thinking?

I know what I want, what is important to me. The moment I begin to speak I am there, present. Breathing in a way which every thought moves me moment to moment. I stand up.

"Thank you!"

I walk towards the door, open it and confidently walk out. They must feel the same thing I do because the letter comes within the following days. They accept me.

But it is a private school. Now I need to find out how to pay for it and how to tell Ruby. With a wish and a wonder, I prepare the best candlelight dinner a man could ever feast on. Coyote stays upstairs with Ally and DeeDee. When Ruby arrives home from the shipyards, he finds me soaking in the tub. Joni Mitchell's *Blue* album wafts through the house.

"Desiree! I'm home."

"Come into the bathroom!" I hear the kathunk of Ruby's lunch pail and his big work boots. He opens the door in all his Apollonian nakedness.

"Yummy!"

"Yummy!" I chime back.

The way to a man's heart, believe me, is through sex and food. Whatever order, you decide. I choose sex first. Hot, hot water, scented candles, big bubbles, soft music, you get the picture. Then the love making. Take all the time you need, follow up with a scrumptious dish, out of a hot oven. Ruby loves my *Coq au Vin* from page. 225 in Fanny Farmer's Cookbook.

Coat the chicken with brown rice flour, fry it in olive oil to brown. Put the chicken in an iron skillet with onions, carrots, potatoes, and mushrooms, add 1 small clove of garlic, 1 bay leaf, 1 tsp of thyme, and 2 cups of Ruby red wine. Bake for 45 minutes at 350 degrees.

Nothing is better than this sizzling dish of chicken coated in a rich-bodied sauce, a salad of spring veggies of tomatoes, arugula, goat cheese and honey-glazed pecans to help set up my plan B.

"I can see this happening very easily," I tell Ruby. "I will find the daycare for Coyote near where Cornish is. I will pick him up after classes. And the way we can pay for it is that I will continue teaching voice lessons to supplement our income. I think this can totally work. Don't you?"

I put my hot skillet of chicken in front of Ruby's dinner dish. I light the candles and unbutton my shirt revealing my ample bosoms one more time. Smiling, I give Ruby a luscious kiss on the lips.

"It may take some other resources in order for it to work," Ruby making sure he gets the last word in.

"Yes, Ruby. By the way, I made you your favorite desert. We can have it in bed." Wink, wink.

Ruby's Choices

On top of all this commotion, Ruby takes a very strange and daunting turn to my big event. He puts in an application to be part of a HUD program. A program to build your own home. Not just one home but four families building four townhouses.

"Are you making things more complicated?"

"No, let's make things more interesting. This is a project for us, as a family."

We are all standing on an empty lot between Jefferson and Cherry Street in the central area. Ruby, Coyote and I, Don and Carolyn, Lakeisha and her two kids, Grace and Jordan and their kid, Joey and another woman, Abbey Moon. An empty lot. Twelve people of diverse backgrounds, ethnicity, political and religious views sharing an economic common ground. None of us have ever had our own home in the city and we are all too poor to buy one. The city of Seattle has linked together with HUD to provide this project for us. To give us a chance to have our own home. But we have to build it, or rather we have to build all four townhouses together. At the end of finishing all four townhouses we will draw lots and get to move in.

There is one catch. You have to work thirty hours a week on top of your own job to make it happen. So I will be going to school, raising a child, and building four homes. A piece of cake! Who says I am not ambitious? Maybe stupid, but just a little.

Ruby puts his long hand out to shake Don Huffman's hand. Don has this zen quality to him with his open face and exquisite eyes.

"Glad to meet you," Ruby says.

"The same." Don smiles back.

The mayor, Charles Royer has just cut the ribbon and a HUD official puts a shovel in the ground and says, "Let's get to work!"

I promise to be there from 3:00 p.m. till dark every weekday. I will pick up Coyote from The Learning Tree Montessori School. We will eat at the Providence Hospital which is across the street from the site. Hospitals always have cheap food. Both Ruby and I will work all day Saturday and Sunday. In the evenings, they are providing special courses in electrical wiring, two-by-four construction, how to run a skill saw without slicing yourself, pound a nail in a count of 1-2-3, and work a router. What's a router?

"I'm quite familiar with building things...," I start to blurt out.

Troy Washington, our job supervisor listens with a seriousness.

"But I've never...," He stops me in mid-sentence and starts to explain the layout of each townhouse.

"The townhouses are connected by a common wall. There will be two bedrooms and a bathroom upstairs. Downstairs there will be a greenhouse..."

"A greenhouse, nice..." I nudge Ruby.

"And an open living and dining room and kitchen on the main floor with a pass through," Troy continues.

This is going to make a difference to Coyote. His own room. A new house. A place he can call home.

Ruby crosses his arms on his chest. He's concentrating hard. He is nodding his head. He's squinting. As I look around the room the other suspects look capable and attentive. We are all working together with a common incentive. Carolyn, Don's wife, seems the most capable woman. She is small, 5 foot 5 inches with sandy blonde hair just past her ears. Her face looks like that of a Californian surfer girl, very brown and rough like someone who spends most of her time outdoors. Her clothes consist of a plaid work shirt with a down vest, faded blue levis and big work boots like a man would wear. Don, on the other hand, looks like an artist. When I shake his hand Don's palm is soft, not like Carolyn's rough and calloused palm. Abbey Moon with her short bob of a haircut and plain sweatshirt and big baggy jeans keeps rolling her eyes and sighing.

"Are you okay?" I ask during the break.

"Well, I've never done this kind of work. I'm a single mom and a teacher."

"Yeah, but you're a teacher. You're smart, You'll get it!"

Lakeisha's kids, Shadoni, a boy, and Akisha, a girl, gravitate to Coyote and Joey, Grace and Jordan's kid. They are standing on the side-lines. Pretty soon you see Coyote take Joey's hand and Coyote pulls him over to where they all start picking up children's wooden hammers and start hammering away on blocks. Two blonde boys and two African-American children learning some valuable skills. Joey turns his head every few minutes making sure his mother and father are acknowledging him. Grace starts handing us out booklets explaining "How we are going to pull this off - building 4 townhouses in one year."

"From the bottom up!" Grace proclaims with her crooked teeth grin and loving eyes.

"We will either become great friends or great

enemies." She chuckles. I chuckle too.

Lakeisha, another single mom, sits in the back talking to an older African-American woman.

"Take your seats, everyone," The tall tower of-a-man Troy Washington bellows. "It's a lot to achieve. You have to put your best foot forward on the weekends. Long days. Some evenings during the week will be devoted to workshops on how to use the tools and how to frame. We need some people to become specialists for the electrical jobs. Some of the work will be subbed out."

"Like what?" Looking confused, Abbey raises her voice.

"The foundation work will be subbed out as well as the plumbing, sheetrock..."

"I'd like to be a specialists for the electrical part," I say, raising my hand and hoping to egg on the other women to join in.

Lakeisha raises her hand and calls out.

"Apparently women have a fear of electricity, getting shocked and all, but if Desiree is willing to figure it out, then count me in!"

Soon Grace is volunteering for framing with Abbey.

Ruby, Don and Jordan pick out their construction belts, adding certain hammers, screwdrivers and squares, and hang them like new-found Christmas ornaments on their belts.

"The girls' hammers are over there," Ruby is happy to point out to us. We pick out our hammers and start feeling the weight of each one and the length.

Holding a hammer is easy enough for me because of all the work I have had to do on my old place in Fruitland. Fruitland seems so far away now. But it doesn't mean I can't visit it for vacations in the summer.

That very next week, an electrical contractor named Brandon Hughs schedules an evening to give Lakeisha and me a private lesson on how electricity flows through circuits. Lakeisha keeps jabbing me in my ribs throughout the workshop and confesses: "I sure do love men in construction. The way they look so rugged and tough."

"How long since you've been with a man?"

"Too long, Desiree. I look at that Brandon and he sure does charge up my sensors."

"Well maybe one of these Saturday evenings you could ask him to explain something in detail when everyone leaves the site."

"Uh-huh, I just might get my nerve up to do that."

A Climb To The Top

Lakeisha and Abbey leave the site every Sunday late at night knowing that all of us will be heading back to our regular jobs, Monday through Friday. Carolyn, Don, Jordan, Grace, Ruby and I start hanging out every Saturday night. Jordan and Grace know Don and Carolyn from being Buddhists. I never thought of Carolyn as a zen character mainly because she is such a hard drinker. We all drink some, others drink more, but hanging out at a bar, playing pool, smoking and just shooting the crap is necessary to wind down from the rigorous agenda we are putting ourselves through.

"Desiree, I need more nails," Don shouts from the roof joints one afternoon.

I begin to climb the ladder to the roof, bringing the extra nails that Don needs. I see that Don is hopping from one roof joint to the next fearlessly. I am noticing that I am starting to panic. Normally I am pretty stable on my feet.

"Hey Don, brought you some nails."

"Bring them over here."

I slowly climb up to one joint and decide that I will wrap my legs around it so I am riding it like a horse.

"You are pretty good at this, Don."

"Can you bring them over here?"

I start to hold on with both hands on the opposite joint and begin to place both feet on the joint I am sitting on and lift my ass up to the sky but about half-way up I begin to freeze.

"I'm feeling a little shaky."

"Don't worry. Don't look down, I'll come and get the nails from you."

Don reaches his hand out to me and I grab on to it hard.

"Look into my eyes." Don continues to hold on to me.

"Okay, I'm looking."

"You and I are going to lift ourselves up together."

"Oh, you think so?"

"Yes Desiree. Remember we can do things together and help each other."

Looking into Don's eyes I feel this intense penetration. Don's eyes are full of compassion. So different from Ruby's eyes. Ruby's eyes always send out the energy of "come on baby, let's go play, let's go have fun, let's get down and sexy together." But Don's eyes reach into my soul and stabilize me.

"Okay Don. I'll do it."

I slowly put one foot on a different rough two-by-four joint. With one hand on Don's hand and one hand on the joint, I take a deep belly breath, lift my ass up, grab Don's other hand and raise my chest and head up into the sky.

"Hold my hand, look into my eyes."

"I am. I am. Is it okay that I don't look around? Can I just keep looking at you?"

"Yes, keep looking at me."

Don's eyes squint and his beautiful compassionate smile beams.

"Desiree, would you pose for me?"

"Pose for you?"

"Can I paint you?"

"Paint me, like spray-paint me?"

"No, can I draw you?"

Attraction on the level of sex is one thing but attraction on the level of spirit is another. Don is the first man who is an attractor of spirit. Maybe it is because we are artists. He's a painter. I'm a singer. We have a deeper connection.

"Why Don, that would be an honor. Ruby's birthday is coming up and I would like to get him something special."

"Uh huh," Don measures one board with his tape measurer and starts to cut one end of it as I help to hold the end.

"You're a watercolorist, right? Most watercolor pictures that I have seen are flowers, lily pads, that sort of thing...but I was hoping you would watercolor me as a nude?"

"Well, I see myself expanding these stereotypes." Don takes a sixteen-penny nail from his carpenter's belt and pulls out his craftsman's hammer.

"Hold that end, Desiree. Put it right here." Don positions my body and hips to hold the support beam into place.

I don't know why but I'm feeling a little warmer when he nudges me in place.

"So would you paint me?"

Don looks up for just a second before he starts to swing his hammer up into position.

"Naked?"

"Yes, naked."

Don hammers one, two and three, and the nail goes in.

"For Ruby, anything."

"Great."

"I will steal some time next week and we will do

a sitting."

     "Is that what they call it? A sitting?"

     "Yes. We'll make a date."

Artists

Don's studio is very small and there are two rooms. One main larger room is filled with easels and paints of red, brown, yellow, blue, green and magenta. Canvases are pulled tight and stacked in every imaginable corner of the room. I feel like I'm at a museum. There are images tacked on the walls of places that Tom has been, places like Mt. Baker, and Oaxaca, and of old barns.

"You'd like Fruitland. Lots of old barns for you to paint."

"Fruitland? Is that where you're from?"

"Yes sir! Fruitland. Where are you from?"

"New Jersey."

"Wow, New York. That's so far away. I've never been past Montana. Montana is God's country. No need to go any further."

"Desiree, you would love New York. Life there is about the arts. Manhattan. There's the Guggenheim Museum. The Metropolitan Opera House. Dance companies like the Alvin Ailey and The Public Theatre where new exciting experimental plays are put on by Joseph Papp."

"It sounds exciting."

As I turn toward Don I see that he is pushing some of his paintings aside so he can open up a small door.

"Come over here and we'll get started."

In the room there is a mattress on the floor with off white satin sheets on it, a small window where the sky shows a bit of sunshine and a brown three-legged stool with a small easel set up in front of it.

"This is where we will create the magic."

I see an impish side to Don. He opens up a large box with several sizes of paint-brushes and baby-food jars full of colors. He pulls out a beige piece of paper that is rectangular in shape and secures it to his easel.

"Lay down there." He points to the mattress.

I start to take my clothes off as he lays a muslin cloth on top of the sheets. I lay my back against the muslin and lift my left arm behind my head to cradle it.

"Can I put my legs like this?"

I leave my right leg straight and bend my left knee so that my left foot is against my right thigh.

"Tree pose."

I chuckle not knowing what he is talking about. Don arranges my long brown hair so that it falls full and side on the muslin.

"Just keep thinking beautiful warm thoughts." Don positions himself by his easel, begins to take a soft brush and strokes the paper slowly and smoothly.

I'm thinking what would it be like to sleep with Don. His soft small hands touching my belly, my breasts and my thighs. I wonder delightfully.

Let's Party!

Halloween is in the air and it is my favorite time of year. The maples are beginning to turn reddish-brown. The roof is done and thank God we are inside doing the wiring. Grace stumbles in at nine a.m. with a cup of joe. I bring my tea in a thermos. Joey and Coyote have their flannel shirts on with long johns underneath. The imaginary whistle blows and we are back at it.

It's Saturday again and some of us have shown up on time. Lakeisha isn't here. Abbey has called in that she is running late. But Grace, Jordan, Don, Carolyn, Ruby and I are accounted for. Ruby, Don, Carolyn and Jordan are installing wiring for the radiant heat for the floors and ceiling in each townhouse. Grace and I are putting up all the boxes for outlets and connecting wires for grounding.

"Desiree, we're having a Halloween Party with my Buddhist friends next Saturday. We want you to come." Grace hands me a yellow wire nob-head to cap the ends of each wire before I shove them all in the box and put the outlet plate on.

"Wowee... what fun! You can always count us in! I got this great idea of wearing all black, skin tight, and using glow tape to design a Picasso painting on my body. It will be cool to glow in the dark and move my body the way the people in the painting seem to move."

"Totally the best idea. I know there will be lots of artists at this party!"

"Wait." I run over to the cassette player and turn up the volume of Talking Head's "Stop Making

Sense."

Grace and I start dancing to the heavy beat and soon shout out:

> *This ain't no party*
> *this ain't no disco,*
> *this ain't no fooling around*

Brandon Hughs' truck honks over the music as he arrives on the scene with Latisha in tow.

"Hey, ladies. How are you doing?" I lower the volume as Brandon and Miss Lakeisha make their grand entrance. I see Lakeisha seems a lot more happier today as she struts herself over to get her carpenter's belt in the tool shed.

"Hey Lakeisha! Have a nice beginning to your weekend?"

"Now, now Desiree, don't you be tempting me to tell you about my Friday night."

"Ah, too bad. I'm always looking for some hot gossip." Grace and I giggle to each other. I turn up my music a bit more as Brandon inspects the men's and Carolyn's jobs.

A Full Moon

Halloween night has arrived and it's official. The full moon is arising. Ruby has made an exceptional costume. He is half man, half woman. I painted half of his face using blush on one cheek, mascara on one set of eyelashes, blue eye shadow on one eye-lid, and ruby red lipstick on half of his lips. His hair is styled with a flip on one side. I have a complete skin-tight black body suit on. Taking glow-in-the-dark white tape, I have arranged a Picasso-ish nude woman on my front side. When I dance in the dark this body will come alive with my movements. My face and head are wrapped in a loose see-through black lace.

We enter Elizabeth Sandveck's house with champagne bottles in hand. Her Seward Park house has an amazing antique interior with dark wood panels and wallpaper that conjure up old aristocratic days. Walls are filled with huge famous paintings. Matisse, Dali and northwest painter Fay Jones plus many more. Beautiful scented candles are everywhere.

"Our hostess is an artist herself. As you can see she has collected beautiful works of famous artists." Grace points to the signature on each painting. I nod my head as though I know who each of these well-known artists are but I don't. Ruby has come in with me but quickly retreats to another section of the house to find friends.

"Grace, there are so many people here."

Someone walks by in a complete zebra costume.

"Hello, Lynn," Grace waves. "That woman is also quite connected in the art world."

The music has already started to create a pulse that the dancers love to hear. I'm passing joint after joint around and the lights are very low so my glow-in-the-dark image is beginning to emerge. A man dressed up as a minotaur with thighs and hooves the size of an elk nudges me.

"Impressive." I whisper in his ear.

"You as well." He snorts his nose and blows his mane. We start to move our bodies in a free-form flow. I feel people behind me and in front of me and by my sides, all drawing closer. There is a man with four eyes. He opens his real eyes then closes them and there are still eyes looking towards me.

"How clever," I yell to him. He grins and I know right away it's Don. He immediately approaches me. His many eyes are locked on to my body. I feel very hot now and so alive. We are in sync. Electrical currents are in full surge. I start to laugh and smile and break the trance as I head towards the kitchen.

"The night is young!" I shout.

Don follows behind me but keeps his distance. He doesn't speak. He lurks behind the door-jamb and slides his head ever so slowly to peer towards me. I find this amusing and giggle and run into another room to see if he will follow. He does. Then he stops and lurks by another door-jamb and repeats moving his head ever so slowly around the corner of the door. I see Carolyn and Ruby talking. I touch both of their hips and try to get them to feel the music filling the room with a contagious beat. I point to Don who is standing perfectly still behind the door-jamb and the three of us make our move.

We extend our arms and hands to signal him to join us. Impish as Don is, he starts to come towards us but drops his costume and becomes the real Don.

The music is on fire and our trio sucks Don in as we grab each other's hips and shoulders and the quartet becomes lost in the groove.

"I love this!" Ruby's eyes are rolling in the back of his head. The LSD that he took earlier is working its mojo. Don pulls out a brownie.

"Want a happy treat?" Don passes it to Ruby, then me and then Carolyn who turns it down, instead pulling out her favorite choice of drug, whiskey.

"Follow me," Don says, pointing.

Carolyn grabs my hips, Ruby grabs Carolyn's hips, I grab Don's hips and we all sashay into a beautiful burgundy bedroom.

"Wow!" I am transported as we enter this room with its velvet wall-paper, crystal chandlers, and a four-post-cherry wood bed that has a canopy of sheer burgundy gauze draped in each corner. Don pulls me onto him as the bed swallows Carolyn and Ruby. We are all kissing each other, touching each other's sweaty bodies, pulling off costumes, pieces of fake hair, moustaches, wigs, French stockings, trousers, capes and women's shirts. The costume pieces are interwoven amongst us as our bodies lay on velvet, satin, lace and leather. Soon we are holding each other in different positions, each sandwiched on top of each other, then all eight hands feeling breasts, buttocks, backs and legs. Mouths sucking lips, penises and vaginas. Everyone entering each other and coming, coming, coming.

"I must be the loudest comer."

Everyone laughs and soon we fall away like flower petals. We look at each other, not saying much, just getting up and starting to dress. One by one we leave the room as though what happened is a fantasy. A film in slow motion going backwards to the beginning of the party.

I am back in the main music room and I see Grace and Jordan. I wave as I part the sea of dancers and travel towards them.

"Where have you been?" Grace asks.

"Oh, exploring..."

Grace hugs me and the three of us finish the last dance of the night.

"Happy Halloween!" we cheer.

Ruby and I lay in bed together. It's Sunday morning and soon we need to get up and pick up Coyote who has gotten enough sleep at DeeDee's house.

"What did you think about last night?" I cuddle up next to Ruby.

"The party?"

"No, what we did with Carolyn and Don?"

"You know me. I'm cool with everything."

"Yes, I know you are but I'm not so sure. I know I don't want to make this a regular thing."

"With them?"

"With anyone. I love making love to you, Ruby. I'm not sure if making love to you and others at the same time would be my thing. You are still my primary relationship, like the books says."

"Desiree, I'm cool with whatever you decide."

"Really?"

"Really."

Building A Home

Every day the site is becoming less of a site and more of the shell of four homes. Every Saturday, Coyote, Ruby and I wake up at seven a.m. in order to be at the site by eight. Rain, snow, or shine, we bundle the kids in Sears special suits like a space outfit that protects them from all weather.

Coyote, Joey, Akisha and Shadoni play with their hammers and nails or serve as our gophers. We take lunch breaks at Providence Hospital. Providence Hospital has the cheapest food, because I couldn't even make hot meals that reasonably. Plus it wouldn't stay hot, and everyone loves a hot meal when it is cold and rainy.

The townhouses are taking shape with their front greenhouses, pass-throughs between the kitchen and dining room, hardwood floors, and radiant heat in the ceilings. The final meeting brings a welcome relief as our foreman announces:

"You don't have to do the sheetrock, everyone." A round of applause erupts. "You don't have to paint. We have subs for that. You are going to get to pick now which unit you'll occupy."

Yays and wows are heard at a high pitch.

"Draw straws!" the kids scream.

This is the defining moment, where what was a dirt hole now has become a home. Coyote keeps tugging on my blue rain pants.

"Can I pick?"

"Yes, of course," Ruby raises Coyote to his shoulder. "Let the kids pick. They have been the most patient."

Joey, Coyote, Akisha and Shadoni run to the front and select their straws.

"Joey, Jordan and Grace, Unit D."

"Coyote, Ruby and Desiree, Unit C."

"Akisha, Shadoni and Lakeisha, Unit B."

"Abbey Moon, Unit A."

"I bet you never thought you'd get here," Troy Washington says clapping. "Next month, all of you will cut the ribbon and these homes will be yours."

I start to cry at the thought of this tremendous undertaking we all set out on. We didn't know one thing about each other but that we were in the same predicament, poor and wanting a home. We came every weekend, even weekday evenings and put aside our own troubles in life to work on a single project. A huge commitment. Whether it was raining or snowing we hammered nails to boards, calloused our hands with wiring, and sometimes even electrocuted our bodies. We perfected angles and stood on beams overlooking the steeples of Baptist churches to set up a permanent structure that was made by our one hundred and twenty hands. Hugs and silences of trials and tribulations are interrupted by "Welcome neighbor, can I help you move in if you can help me?" Surely nothing would stop me from nurturing these friendships that formed ten strong months ago.

The Move

Coyote has been in his room packing his Legos, Value Village T-shirts and pants.

"Dad, I'm not taking the bed. You have to get me a real bed."

"How about a bunk-bed?'

"A bunk bed is two beds in one, right?"

"Yes. One for you and one for a friend."

"Any friend I want to come and stay over?"

"Of course."

"Thanks, Dad!" Coyote runs and jumps into his dad's arms.

"It's okay if we get a few new things or at least some garage sale items?"

"Yes. We need to leave the milk cartons behind." Ruby winks at me as I opened Coyote's door.

"I'm so excited and proud of us for doing this!" Ruby grabs me around my waist as Coyote slips in between us.

"I can't wait to make love to you, Desiree, in our own home." Ruby whispers into my ear.

"Let's load up the Dodge Dart. Home of our own, here we come!"

The Learning School

Coyote kisses me goodbye as I drop him down at the front door of The Learning Tree Montessori School. I see Bill Bergman, the Acting Department Head at Cornish College coming up the walk.

"Hey Bill! Your daughter goes to school here too?"

Coyote and Bill's daughter run into the school together.

"Why yes. Why are you here?"

"I'm dropping off my little boy, Coyote."

"You have a son?" Bill's face shifts suddenly from delighted to perplexed.

"Yes, I do. See you at class."

At Cornish College of the Arts, Lena Swift's class is the most imaginative. I feel like I'm a young child again. We perform a ritual based on the different stages of the beginning of life.

"Class, today you are going to be creating the seven stages of man." Lena begins.

"Lay down on the floor." Now my eyes are looking at the enormous cathedral ceilings of this old church we are working in.

"Breathe deeply." I begin to relax using all my low belly singing movements. My mind falls deeper into a meditative space. With cues from Lena, I start to see images about my birth.

"The first stage is the beginning of life." I breathe deeper and my subconscious imagination takes over. I see diamonds glistening as my limbs stretch.

"No words, just movements, class."

My body responds to these images in my subconscious as I open up and spill forth into the world. I start to make sounds and it seems very necessary.

"Sounds are alright. No words though."

My feet and arms are trying to understand how to move. My head is trying to figure out how to hold itself up. I drag my body around until I lift my lower body up. Now I'm taking in the world around me as my body becomes erect. Lena Swift studied at the famous theatre international school in Paris which was developed in 1956 by Jacque LeCoq. The courses emphasize body movement and the dynamics of space. We study natural elements like animals, sounds, and looking at the world around us from the outside in.

"Today's class is on archetype characters that are used in mask work." Lena turns her back to us and puts on a beautiful white mask. As she turns around to us her body shape changes. She doesn't speak a word. Her body moves and reveals emotions from this mask by just a slight change.H My mind wanders to the past when Terry and I were Pierrot and Pierrette. It seems so long ago.

Lena turns her back to us and quickly takes the mask off and puts it gently on the floor with the face up.

"The energy of the mask is powerful. You will never put it down on the floor with the face on the ground. Never. You will never speak while the mask is on. Learn who these characters are. Zanni, Brighella, Pierrot, Coviello, Pedrolino..."

I look out at the huge tree outside the class window. I wonder what Terry is doing now.

"Desiree?" Lena calls.

"Yes, Lena?" My body becomes rigid.

"I'd like to meet with you after class if you have a moment." She gives me a mask. I look at its facial features.

"Desiree, what does it suggest to you?" I put my back to the audience and place the mask on my face and turn instantly back to the audience. I start to maneuver my body in large movements.

"Is the character fat or skinny?" Lena suggests as I move. "What does the long nose make you want to do?" Everyone in the class starts to laugh at what I am feeling and displaying. My nose leads me. It has become the strongest, most powerful area of my body. I lunge forward and sway sideways, graceful like a penguin, using my nose as a sensor. Elegantly, I walk very erect but very slowly, exploring this movement for what seems like about five minutes. Lena clanks a bell and I turn my back away from the audience and remove the mask, carefully placing it with its face upwards as I return it to Lena.

"Nice work, Desiree."

There is something about being silent. I feel very comfortable in this class. As I leave, Lena motions me into the gymnasium, where not one single person is using the space.

"Desiree, you have a child, don't you?"

"Yes. Why?"

"Well, this might create a problem in your commitment to the program."

"Why would it create a problem?"

"Bill and I would like to discuss this with you tomorrow after school. Meet us at his office."

What's a fair education? Or even better, what's a

fair education for a woman? Okay, even better, what's a fair education for a mother with a child?

Bill and Lena have decided to call this meeting today. I arrive at Bill's tiny office. Stacks and stacks of paper are piled up two feet high on either side of his old desk. A grand cathedral window looms behind Bill's swirling chair. Lena sits cramped on a folding chair strategically placed in a corner next to him. I am thinking maybe I should have brought Coyote along because he is so beautiful to look at and wins many people over with his smile.

Bill pontificates.

"In the real world we need you to understand the commitment that one needs to make it in the theatre world."

"Excuse me," I begin. "The real world is not Cornish Institute. I am the product of the real world. I am older and have much more life experience."

Lena interrupts. "But you have a child."

"Both of you have children." Bill looks at Lena. Lena takes in a breath.

"That's not the point. What if your son gets sick?"

"Lena, you have a husband, right? Bill, you have a wife! I have Ruby and he will be there. Besides children have universal mothers and fathers as well."

Lena curls her upper lip and lower lip into her mouth and presses down hard. Bill obviously is not going to speak at all.

"As I see it, maybe it's better to only educate kids right out of high school than older adults with responsibilities and struggles. No mommies and daddies paying for our college education. Those young kids have been educated to say 'yes'."

"I am here to challenge you to give me the best

education possible for a woman who happens to have a child."

Bill's phone rings. His smile registers relief.

"Hello, Bill Bergman. Yes, Reagan?" Bill's voice has a slight hint of concern. "I will be right over."

I stare at Bill but he jumps up from his desk trying to find his canvas satchel.

"Reagan? Is she okay?"

"Well, I'll let you both go now." Bill rushes out as Lena stands up.

"I'll need to get back to a rehearsal for a class assignment. By the way, Lena, I love your class." I stand up and leave the office.

A Teacher

It's another rainy day in Seattle but in the Central Area, it's the day of loving Christ. Ruby and I have never discussed much about religion. I believe that religion is the nature of life. Nature being trees, plants, animals, primitive states of existence untouched and uninfluenced by civilization. Natural. Real. And I believe in some of what civilization has influenced on us. It's something I can hold on to. I see that every person should be respected, and so should planets, plants and animals. It is my duty to find happiness in each day that I wake up and to spread that happiness to others.

Outside the greenhouse windows, we see a parade of religious folks in their Sunday fineries. Large hats and heels clip clop on down the sidewalk to the big white church called The Baptist Church. The organ is immense and swinging the sounds of old time religious hymns to the congregation inside as well as out. Women's voices tower over the men as the shouting and clapping ignite a chorus of "Yes, Sister!" "Amen!" and "Glory Be!" I close my eyes and start singing and swaying to tunes that have familiar melodies though I do not have the words to unite with them. Several hours pass and the congregation tumbles out of its door spilling out the salvation they have found in their hearts. I walk on by to relish in that moment. I bow my head and say, "Hello!" Many come up and say "Hello, you are the singer, aren't you? Is this your boy?"

"Yes, I teach voice lessons. And this is Coyote."

"What?"

"Singing lessons."

"Well, we will pass it on to the choir director. Keep up the singing. We love to hear music in the neighborhood."

"Certainly." I wave and walk on down the street with Coyote by my side. Walking down to our grocery store, we notice homes that have seen a sadder kind of life. Many homes were regal in their heyday but with constant rain, wind and shine their paint jobs are wearing thin. Wrought-iron designs encase every window on the ground floor. People walk by with less finery on the weekdays than Sundays. Our existence is noticeable. Coyote and I are a minority in a sea of majority. People look at us and walk on by with both friendliness and unfriendliness. Coyote looks up at me.

"Ma, does Lakeisha put on make-up?"

"What do you mean?"

"Do they put brown on their skin?"

"Why do you think that?" Coyote suddenly becomes silent and his eyes become withdrawn.

"Oh! You think the people here put make-up on their white skin? People are born in this world with all sorts of colors. There are white-skinned people. There are brown-skinned people. Some people have other colors or pigments in their skin coloring. Basically we are all human beings but we have different colors, different cultures, different places that we come from."

"Where is Lakeisha from?"

"Lakeisha is African-American. Her family came from Africa."

"I know where Africa is."

"Good for you. Remember, no matter what color you are, your color is never better that anyone else's."

The Singer

Money is tight so I've started to send out notices in The Rocket newspaper.

> *Sore throat? Small Range?*
> *Learn to sing without hurting your voice.*

I've got my first student. It's a girl who is part of a sister's act. Her name is Siri of the Blaine Sisters. Their style is alternative folk rock. All originals. She calls me.

"We're playing down at the OK Hotel tonight."

"Great. I will come by and see you."

I walk over to the kitchen where Ruby is devouring his veggie sandwich of avocado, sprouts and cheese.

"Hey Ruby, since I'm teaching I thought it would be great to see my students and give them feedback. The Blaine Sisters are playing tonight. Do you want to go?"

Ruby holds a carton of milk and opens the top of it.

"That is a great idea. I'm in. You may get more students by connecting with other bands that are playing around in the Seattle music scene."

Karol and her sister, Siri take the stage in an old brick building down under the viaduct across from the pier. The OK Hotel is a happening music venue. It seems everyone who is a famous musician is playing there. Ruby and I gravitate towards a long line that is forming to get in.

"Ruby, why are people wearing sunglasses at

night?" "Oh, they want to be celebrities."

"When did flannel shirts become a fashion statement?"

"Since you and I started wearing them." I jab him in the ribs.

As the lights go down, I pull out my notebook. I stand underneath an antique gold wall sconce that shines just enough light on my notepad. Karol and her sister, Siri come out on stage holding guitars.

"Are they twins?" Ruby says low.

"No, they're sisters."

The two of them have a really sweet blend to their voices. Their songs speak to me as a woman. Ruby sees a pool table in the distance and wanders over to it. He waves hello to his old friend, Eric, an albino and points towards the table.

I'm jotting down questions about their expressions and emotions for the songs. Where do you begin with this song? What happens the moment before you start singing? Who is the song about? What kind of a relationship? What kind of emotions are going on in this section? In the chorus, what do you want? I listen intently to their lyrics. What are the most important words that you should be stressing? There are times that you should look at the audience but you should look at each other too. Suddenly someone taps me on my shoulder.

"Desiree, you are writing up a storm."

"Studying acting now has given me so much insight to becoming a better performer, Ruby. I want to pass all this knowledge on to my students."

"You are going to be a great teacher." Ruby bends down and kisses me on the cheek and heads back to the pool table.

The Blaine Sisters sing and play for about 50

minutes. I look over my shoulder and see that Ruby's face looks delighted he must be winning. The girls start to gather up their instruments, so I go over to both of them.

"Great show, girls. When I see you at your next lesson, Siri, I'll give you feedback."

"Really nice of you to come see us. I hope I did okay."

"You did great!" I smile and put my note book in my purse and head over to grab my man.

"Ruby, are you ready to go back home?"

Tapping the eight ball in, he pulls me tight to his side.

"You're my celebrity."

The next day at Cornish, I start to put up flyers in the drama and music departments advertising my singing classes. It doesn't take long for the phone to start ringing with people inquiring about lessons.

More Bands

Thunder is shouting across the skyscape. Clouds are lighting up in bursts of white neon every seven seconds. I'm standing in a classroom at Cornish. I have a new student coming and I thought that since I had rehearsals late that he could come here to Cornish. Damn, the lights in the building just went out.

There's a knock at the door.

"Yes, I'm here."

I open the door and a silhouette of a man is standing there. He is not very tall.

"Are you Desiree, the voice teacher? I'm Ben."

"Yes I am, even though you can't see me so well. I know this is awkward and strange but I can still give you a voice lesson. It will just be in the dark."

"Hey I'm game. Siri said great things about how you can help people like me."

"Well, let's give it a try and see what you think? Follow me slowly over here. We are going to a piano."

I make sure all the chairs were out of the way.

"We are going to record your lesson so you can go back and hear the difference we are going to make with your voice."

"I'm in a band, Skinyard. My mother was an opera singer. She was singing all the time around the house. She showed me a few things as I got older, when I was willing to listen."

"What don't you like about your voice?"

"I want to scream with it and still be able to keep my range."

"Do you have any aspirations with your band?"

"We want to take it all the way."

"Do you know where your diaphragm is?"

"It's here."

We both laugh. I can hardly see where he is pointing to on his body.

"I am a pretty physical teacher. So if you don't mind I am going to show you where your diaphragm is and what it does when you sing."

I take my hands and place them where his ribs and sternum meet. I follow his lower ribs where they separate and continue down on both sides, and then along the sides of his body and around to his back.

"The ribs that I am touching are where the diaphragm is attached all the way around you."

"That's pretty amazing," he says in his rich baritone voice.

"Think about this. Imagine a piece of paper. That is how thin your diaphragm is and it completely dissects you in half."

"So it's like a pizza in the middle of me."

"Exactly."

"Wow, I never knew that."

"Now it is your turn, Ben. Open your hands as big as you can. I am going to put them on my rib cage area and you can feel what I do when I sing."

Ben opens his hands and places them on my body.

"When I take a breath through my nose, it opens up the rib cage in front and along the sides. When I take my breath next through my mouth, it will open the rib cage in the back and my abdomen muscles will pooch out."

"Your rib cage really goes out bigger than mine."

"Now feel what it does when I sing."

I take my breathe in and sing a phrase from 'Caro Mio Ben.'

"My mom used to sing that song."

"Really?"

"And yes your ribs stayed out the whole time."

"Right. They stayed out. Do you do that?

"No, I don't think so."

"Now you are going to lay down on the rug here and I have this Shakespeare book here..."

"Are we going to recite sonnets to each other?" We both start to chuckle.

"No, we are going to do a breathing exercise. Lay down on your back with your knees up and I am going to place the book below your ribs, down to your groin area."

"Oh, that's a heavy book."

"Yes, you need some weight to push your abdominal muscles out against. Take a sniff through your nose and lift the top part of the book up and now take a gulp of air through your mouth and lift the bottom of the book out and hold it out."

I feel the book lift up and out. Ben is holding it out.

"Keep holding it out. 20 seconds, 30 seconds, 40 seconds, 50 seconds."

Ben exhales. He grabs my hand which has been on the book the whole time.

"I felt them. I felt my abs. It is like I have to make my abs strong going outward, instead of inward."

"That is so cool, that you get this."

Ben still is holding my hand. "I love singing."

I start to take the book off his stomach.

"Me too."

Loving Coyote

Coyote, Ruby and I have settled into our new space. The piano has a place near the greenhouse window. I've draped my Grandmother's shawl on it. The hardwood floors are warm to our feet which is such a joy every morning when we wake up. We've started to arrange our comfy chairs and a couch around the piano. The pass-through to the kitchen shows off Johnny Crush's roll up cabinets that he made for my birthday. They are made from oak and look so special because no other townhouse has a kitchen like ours. I chose a cobalt blue for the counters. The linoleum has Japanese blue bamboo designs on it for the floor. We bought a simple shiny black table for four and it can also fold out to accommodate 8 people for dinner parties. Upstairs, we have our master bedroom in front of the house. But the bathroom is my creative idea. I painted it all black even the ceiling. Glossy black. The white toilet and white tiled shower cast off this grand impression. Coyote's room is next to it with bunk beds that Ruby and Coyote built. Purple rectangles and yellow triangles with red and green slats coordinate the Lego décor of his bedroom.

"How do you like your new home, Coyote?" Ruby hugs him close.

"I like it a lot but I would like a rabbit and a bird as well."

"Well I guess I'll pull it out of my hat and see what we can find." They start hopping like rabbits.

Ruby starts to turn but stops in his tracks.

"I know. Let's go visit Linda Fino's house."

Linda is the patron of animals. Her animals might be out of fabric and iron but I'm sure she'll point us to the right place. On the corner of 18th and Madison sits Linda Fino's pink car and pink house with a large circular porch. When the door opens, the one and only Linda stands squarely in front of us. Her massive orange hair springs wildly from her scalp.

"Oh you guys! I am so happy you came to visit."

To the right of her front door is another door. Inside that door, she leads us into a sanctuary that is all black inside.

"Linda, you are a soul color sister."

The high ceilings show exposed wooden beams that have stuffed ravens with red eyes hanging down from them. Several black iron chandeliers with candles hang down into the ceiling air space. Nigel, her big mutt of a dog barks uproariously. Our eyes gaze up and down, over and around all the amazing artwork in each of Linda's rooms. Then we find ourselves in an all white room with concrete chickens. Some of them are laying down with their tiny feet up and some of them are standing on their feet. Everywhere there is a white powdery dust.

"What are you up to?"

"I am looking for a rabbit." Coyote quickly answers Linda.

"A rabbit. Well, I have just the rabbit for you."

Coyote replies quickly again.

"No, it has to be real."

"Is this real enough for you?" Linda opens the back door of her pink house revealing a back yard filled with high green grass and a tiny pink house with very plump white rabbits with pink noses.

"See there they are."

Coyote pulls us towards the rabbits. He bends down low to the ground as all the rabbits shy away from him. But there is one that decides it will be bold and jumps towards Coyote.

"Thumper, Thumper, come here." Coyote wiggles his little finger through the wire fence. Coyote yanks us both down towards the one he has selected.

Daily Life

Between teaching, going to Cornish and taking care of Coyote and Ruby's needs, I'm feeling pretty fulfilled. The first year acting students are mostly older, which means they are not just right out of high school. Our group has been vocal about that "when you get in the real world..." line that some of the professors are using. We are already in the real world and we know how to operate in it and we are here to learn. We talk amongst ourselves about which teachers are valuable and which are not and what they can do to make the program stronger. I've been focused on doing the work, and being part of a team.

When I go home, I switch hats and I am there for Coyote. I fix good vegetarian dinners such as lentil loaf with a mushroom gravy. My copy of "Diet for a Small Planet", my Fannie Farmer Cookbook, The Moosewood Cookbook, and The Tassajara Bread Book are my savory friends. They keep my imagination fresh and inventive. Ruby and I are happy, watching Coyote grow up with his other new pet, Shadow the cockatiel. The rabbit, Thumper, is sweet and hoppity around the living room but Shadow is amazing. She flies everywhere. I've decided cages shouldn't be where animals live except for the rabbit.

"Shadow, we're home," Coyote calls as soon as we come in the back door. Shadow flies and lands on Coyote's head.

"Did you have a good day, Shadow? Such a pretty bird, such a pretty bird." Coyote repeats over and over.

I take my thumb and index finger and stroke her small fragile head. I've never seen such a lover in a bird. She walks from the top of Coyote's head over to his shoulder, then over to his collar bone, the whole time Coyote runs up and down the stairs putting toys away and getting ready for homework. When Coyote sits at the dining table, Shadow snuggles under his chin and purrs there like a kitten.

"Hum a song for Shadow." Coyote softly sings the Kookaburra song and we stroke Shadow's feathers of gray and white.

"Sometime you have to take the clear casing off her feathers. That will make the feathers softer and freer for her." I show Coyote how the hard casings can be easily broken with his thumb and second finger.

"Coyote, you are such a lover of animals."

"Ma, can we have a animal farm? There will be goats, chickens, rabbits, birds, dogs and cats."

"Coyote, do you want to go to Fruitland this spring?"

"Fruitland? Can we bring Shadow?"

"Maybe but let's first take her in the car a few times and see if she likes it."

"Ok Ma. We'll take her to the store."

That night after we finish dinner, we get Shadow to play 'Hide and Seek.' The rabbit definitely does not understand what we were doing, but Shadow does. Coyote and I hide up in my bedroom closet. We leave Shadow downstairs in the greenhouse.

"Now call out. Yell out so Shadow will come and find us," I whisper to Coyote.

"Shadow, come and find us!" Coyote calls joyously.

"Open the door, just a crack." I say.

We can hear Shadow's wings fluttering up the stairs, into Coyote's room, and then down the corridor to the bathroom and then into my room.

"Shh! Be quiet. She is here." I signal to Coyote. Coyote's eyes grow large and he puts his hand over his mouth. He starts to giggle. Shadow is hovering at the door. Just waiting. Coyote slides open the door.

"Shadow, you found us." We cheer as Shadow takes her position on the crown of Coyote's head.

A Respect for Acting

Fred Conrad commands attention. His short black hair and shrewd Italian face reminds me of a Mediterranean sailor. His olive skin and piercing eyes can sometimes take your breath away. Sarah and Alex, my new acting friends agree that he is not bad for the eyes.

"Respect for Acting by Uta Hagen. Everyone must read this," he challenges us one day in class.

"Commit to creativity!" He shouts as he enters the room. I write down every word coming from his mouth.

"Think art, make art, love what you do. Today, we are going to do the blind exercises."

Sarah, Alex, and I look up and notice that Fred has arranged many chairs as obstacles all over the open area of the acting room.

"Even though it is broad daylight out each person will be moving around with someone as a guide, but each person will also move around on their own, blindfolded."

Sarah's mouth registers a big "Oh my God!" We all gather around Fred as he chooses partners first.

"Desiree and Sarah. Desiree will be blindfolded first and Sarah, you lead her."

Before I put the blindfold on, I feel instantly trusting of Sarah to help me navigate the room. I place one hand on her shoulder and begin to slowly move forwards and backwards with no words spoken, just touch. Sarah watches behind me and around me, always keeping watch that I won't trip over anything.

"Desiree and Sarah, you may stop now. Great connection between the two of you. Class, did you notice how there was constant trust?" Everyone claps as I release the blindfold and I notice we are on the other side of the room with Sarah smiling.

"For Wednesday's class, I want a monologue on hunger."

"What do you mean by that?" Sarah raises her hand.

"We all have a physical hunger inside us, but we also can have emotional hunger, intellectual hunger, sexual hunger..."

Joe Blunt raises his hand.

"You want us to write our own monologues?"

"Yes, Joe. But I want you to perform them as well. I want to know each of you deeper."

Alex winks at me and I put my hand over my mouth as I chuckle quietly. Sarah lowers her eyes, trying not to laugh out loud.

The stage has a center spot light. I am covered up with black linen. It is draped over me so that only me eyes can be seen. I am sitting on my butt with my knees close to my chest. My arms and hands are stretched out holding a silver tray. Sarah clicks the tape recorder and my monologue begins to play:

"*You know why I love being a waitress? Because of food. I love food. I love to serve food. It makes people happy. I serve mankind in my own special way. The world comes to me. I open my arms to them and for an hour or two, their lives become mine. It is important for people to eat. When people are hungry, I give them fast service. Hunger can do some strange things to people.*"

One of my hands begins to shrivel down on this line. The tray falls to the ground. My other hand reaches out as if I am begging for food.

"Some people get very slow and can hardly move. Like these pictures of hungry people in India. Then there are the people who get very fast and bitchy. Those people you have to serve quickly or else. But do you know what I like the best about food?"

I take both of my hands now and start to pull the black linen up so that my bloating belly is exposed.

"It is the leftovers. I take as much as I can and fill my bags full so I won't go hungry for the week. Waitressing is the most rewarding job for me."

The spotlight goes out. Sarah stops the tape recorder. The rest of the class claps in approval. Fred walks to the front of the stage as I jump off it and join my fellow actors in the audience.

"Did the performance move you?"

"Yes. I was captivated by her contorted body," Alex blurts out.

"The slow movements highlighted certain sections of the piece," Joe Blunt joins in.

"I like the juxtaposition of a waitress who has constant food around her and the creature in black who appears to be starving," Deanna comments.

"Nice job, Desiree. It is interesting that you chose not to speak," Fred responds.

"Since I have been working with Lena, I prefer to not speak."

"Continue on your exploration," Fred comments

as he looks at the clock on the wall and the class starts to gather up their belongings. Leaving Fred's class fills me with wanting to discover more. My connection to the world and others seem to be opening up.

Ruby Clouds

Lightning strikes through the grey billowy clouds but Ruby cocoons himself at the kitchen table. I am observing. He's been still for quite awhile. He reads constantly. Even if it's not a book, he reads loose paper, or carton of cereal, milk, yogurt, you name it. I am feeling something simmering inside me.

"Talk to me!"

"I don't know," Ruby looks up and immediately his eyes dart down at a scrap of newspaper again. "Not now. I want to eat my lunch in quiet."

That statement makes me stop and recoil into observing. It is his shit, not mine. I am doing my own thing. He has to figure it out. I know the pattern. I will ask him in 3 days. Again, I will ask the question: "What's going on?" "How are you feeling?" Emotions or words about emotions don't come easy to him. He is very intellectual. I'm the emotional one. But I get anxious when he doesn't talk to me. I feel abandoned. I need a shared word or two to be able to still be "we" instead of "me."

Back in Fruitland

I've decided I need a little down time this summer.

"Boys, I'm going to Fruitland. I'm going to vacate for a couple of weeks and then I'll be back."

The boys look at each other and nod "Yeah!" enthusiastically because that's what boys do. They have fun together doing the man thing while the women are away.

Driving to Fruitland will land me there in about five hours if I have the pedal to the metal. Oh, my favorite spots on Highway 90 are Snoqualmie Pass, and Ellensburg, a windy city. Then onward to Vantage and the Columbia Gorge which is just barren dirt with sage-brush tumbling along. I love Soap Lake and the Ephrata area where the Russians have settled, mudding themselves and baking by the lake. Down the highway, Sun Bank, Coulee City and Almira are places I used to ride with a friend on his souped-up Harley-Davidson. At Creston City, you take a left and drive on through the Colville Indian Reservation.

"Whoo, wheee! Where are my dogs?" I reminisce.

The hawks are racing with me and now the swallows dart back and forth across my path.

"There's the Bible Camp!" I turn right and see the camp ahead. Fruitland Bible Camp was founded by Rev. Edwin Torgerson in 1943. It is a camp with tents, cabins and RV facilities for people of all ages for ministry retreats.

"Aha! No Biblers. Let's take a left here and let

the Lord shed a light on you."

The next right puts the car on a gravel road. There is green grass swirling as the wind hits it and the sun is starting to cast a yellow light against the ponderosa pines as it sets. I'm taking another left past the Gramer's house.

"Oh my God! Lookee. Johnny has built a honey house."

It is a huge yellow metal building that looks like a hanger but knowing Johnny it is where he is storing all his bee-hives and extractor.

I honk and idle for awhile but no one comes a running out. So I forge ahead onto the old road, slowing down for bumps and rocks. Up ahead should be the neglected apple trees on someone else's property.

"Oh those old apple trees are still trying to survive. That's good."

The alfalfa field below the pond is three feet high and is covering up my old road. I can hardly remember the way in.

"Oh well, I'll burn a new one."

I cross my fingers, hoping I won't hit a small shrub in the road. It could take out my exhaust pipe again. Barreling through the field of hay, past the thimble berries and overgrown rose bushes, I see the end of the road opening to a huge pasture.

"There she is." The eight-sided octagon cabin still is perched high in the pristine ravine of beautiful tall grasses welcoming me home.

"Ahhh, the sun has turned your wood burnt red. What a sight for sore eyes."

Relishing the moment, I go to the door. The padlock number? Shoot. I can't remember it. But I know I scribbled it on one of the logs by the orange blossom bush. I walk over and behind the overgrown orange blossom bush are the numbers scribbled on the bottom log.

"24,6...-30, right? Ahh, that's the number. Amazing. After so many years."

The white door with a long window pane in its center creeks open, slowly revealing my uninhabited cabin. The white and black tiles on the floor manage to look still brand new even though there is a light dusting on them. The pale green wood cook-stove needs some degreasing.

"Did I really leave it like that?" I go over and open up the fire box. There is still kindling and firewood. All I need to do is light a match.

"Might as well light it. It will keep off the chill."

After I light the fire, I go to the center of the log cabin and stand before the tree trunk. I remember how I stripped all the bark off and made it into the backbone of my home. There are pictures tacked on it. A few postcards from friends visiting faraway places and lovely poems about the saga of Ruby and Desiree.

The piano that I wrapped up tightly in plastic and covered with old Indian blankets awaits my inspection. The plastic has gotten brittle and it looks like mice might have eaten the bottom plastic at the floor. I retrieve a black plastic garbage bag from my backpack. Taking my yellow handkerchief, I first place it over my nose and mouth and then tie a big knot behind my head. Pulling and ripping piece after piece of plastic, the details of the Navaho blankets appear. Brown triangular shapes with black arrows above them are in perfect condition. Taking the blankets off one by one, I have to decide where I should put them away from the dusty surroundings.

I'll place them in the car until I can get everything wiped down. Coming back into the cabin, I get an old rag and bucket. Filling it with vinegar and water that I brought along, I start to wipe the pearl keys. Each black and white key I gently wipe to see if they are still playable.

"Slightly out of pitch but relative," I say to myself. "I am sure I can find someone to tune her up again. The cherry wood shines up real good."

I wipe and wipe till the piano looks gorgeous. Sitting down, I start to put my fingers down to play.

"I wonder where I put the piano books?" Glancing behind, I see the cabinet that Thames and Vince had given to me. The cabinet is unique. It had been built especially for sheet music. Shelves of single sheet pieces and collections are laid out waiting for me to pick up and play. I set my bed up down on the main floor next to the French doors until I can clean the upstairs.

Musical Thoughts

"Good morning Classical Spokane. Today, I have picked a most beautiful piece of music for you, Maurice Ravel's Pavanne for a Dead Princess." My morning clock radio blares out the voice of Mr. Vince Windnam.

"Oh my golly, Vince. How perfect to hear you."

It's morning time in Fruitland. Maurice Ravel is in the air. Outside ravens are crowing, chickadees are chirping, bees are buzzing and flies are landing. I boil up some hot water on my cook stove. I open up my old Chinese canister and spoon up some green tea. I spread my drapes of old sarongs and look out the windows to the north, south and east to see if Mr. Moose, Miss Deer or Mr. Elk have trudged by to visit.

"Where are you out there?"

I take my cup of tea and start to mosey outside to sit in the field and write. But Vince interrupts my mind as a French horn plays. Vince was a French horn player who accompanied me when I sang down in the Hangman Valley at the end of Coeur D'Alene Street. Vince is an educated man who was the first seat French horn player of the Spokane Symphony. When I attended music school at Fort Wright College with Richard Hampson, Karen Bairsley and Linda Kaple, Vince taught us about 20th century music. That was the time I began my long love affair with music and with Vince. A musician with black hair below his shoulders and large bookish glasses which sat studiously on his narrow nose. I always listened attentively to his melodious and deep voice. Vince had Thames, his sweetheart and Thames let both of us know at the beginning that we would never have a chance to sleep together. Our bodies were musician's bodies, fine tuned and what a vivacious third movement we could have created.

"It would be nice to visit Vince again while I'm here."

It is starting out already a warm morning. The air is blowing through the wild grasses, purple vetches and prickly hound's foot. Hearing the creek below on the north side and looking out into the pines that circle the cabin, I hear a hummingbird whisk by.

"Better fill up the feeder!"

My mind rattles off the long list for the day. Go for a walk to see how the beavers and the honey bees are doing. See if Johnny will take a plunge in the Columbia River with me. Get a few things for the cabin. The wear and tear on the cabin hasn't been too bad while I was gone, but I had left without painting the windows trims properly. Thank God, my piano was all wrapped up in the plastic but the mice sure have been enjoying free range of my home. Better take control. My outhouse needs a new hole dug. But first, I'm going to lounge in my chair, feed the birdfeeder, sip my tea, eat a apple and enjoy being alone and quiet. My mind wanders as I listen to the wind blowing across my pasture. Would it be better to stay here in Fruitland and be with nature or go back and be in the big city? Just breathe and see where it takes me.

I get up early the next day and head for Spokaloo. I drive down towards the bridge where the Colville Indians are and across the bridge to Fort

Spokane and then towards Davenport. Before Davenport there is this exquisite little white church welcoming all visitors, and past it, is the tiny town of Egypt. Onwards to Highway 25 to Spokaloo, the vast open skies are showing all the signs of summer weather ahead. Spokaloo is still the same as always, trying to be a town of prominent culture mixed with hobos, trailer trash and Deadheads.

As I turn on Vince's radio station KPCX, I decide to pay a surprise call on Mr. Vince Windnam. While I fill up my car with gas, the attendant shows me a phone book and I find that the radio station is on Division Street towards Deer Park. I've got the address and start to whistle as the cross streets whizz by.

"There it is," I say gleefully to myself. I slow down and pull over to park.

I'm glad I'm wearing my favorite cowgirl hat of white straw adorned with coral inserts on leather strapping. I am also wearing my favorite gauzy Indian shirt, with a delicate floral pattern, and a short denim skirt. I look good. Every girl should look good when seeing an old male friend. I knock on the old wooden door with a glass pane etched on it "Classical Music Station KPCX."

As I slowly open the door and peer around the small reception room I see Vince talking to the receptionist I presume. They both look up but Vince looks with his quizzical eyes saying, "Oh my God, it's you!"

"Yes, it's me!"

"Oh, I get mind flashes of you from time to time wondering where Desiree's saga has taken her."

"Well, right here back to you." I walk up to him and give him a hug.

"Let's go somewhere. I have a break but need to be back for the afternoon show."

We drive towards Riverside to sit at the park overlooking the Spokane Falls.

"I brought some goodies to eat for lunch."

"Me too. Let's share."

Sitting at the park with my yellow gingham table cloth and containers of hummus, cucumber slices, carrot sticks, goat cheese spread and flaxseed crackers, we began like we had never been apart.

"What are you doing now, Miss Desiree?"

"Oh, I'm with a man named Ruby and I have a beautiful boy, Coyote."

"I'm with a singer, Susan, now and I have two boys."

"No Thames?"

"No."

We stare into each other's eyes.

"You know Thames never wanted us to..."

"Yes, I know, and neither would Susan." Vince puts his fingers on my lips.

"We are so good together." I lean in closer to his face.

"I know and I cheat a little." Vince winks at me.

"How do you cheat, Vince Windnam?"

"I play love symphonies for you on the radio, hoping that you will hear them."

"Ohhh!" I sigh.

I beam with such pride and love for Vince. His way was to play the symphonies as a sign of his undying love for me all these years.

I bend over and gently kiss his cheek.

The Huckleberry Hills

I've decided to get up and do a hike today. Haven't had the chance to put on my old Red Wing hiking boots and grab my walking stick in so long.

It's another beautiful expansive morning in my sweet Fruitland. The clouds are stacked on top of each other but the sun keeps playing hide and seek amongst these beautiful clouds. My favorite hiking spot is up the ravine towards Bria's cabin and around it further up in the Huckleberry Mountains. I slip into my old blue jeans and rayon plaid button-down cowboy shirt and place my moth-eaten cowboy hat on my head. As I wander up through the tall grasses, I notice scat on the ground. It looks pretty fresh and of course it is cougar scat. I know a cat is out there because I heard her screaming last night. It's like a baby screaming. At least I have my whistle. They don't like the sound and it does scare them.

"Damn, the old trail is so overgrown with wild rose bushes. Can't seem to make headway."

I keep whacking the bushes down and eventually make a path. Clearly Mama Bear has been through here too, probably munching on some of those apple trees down below as well as a few of them on Bria's place. At the top of the ravine sits an old cabin and barn of Don, who owns the Clydesdale horses. The immense creatures worked his land but Don is gone now and the cabin and barn still are standing. To the right of his cabin, down a dirt road full of pot holes, is Bria's cabin. Bria is Fruitland's kindergarten teacher. She has a large never-finished log cabin. Never finished because Tom, her mate, flew the coop. Tom was a scammer. He tried every scam to make money. If you had listened to him, you would have wondered how he never could figure out he was the one being scammed. He lusted for the strike-it-rich fantasy, but never got his riches. Bria now lives in a half-built house waiting to find someone to complete it. No car is in sight so she must be gone. As I recall, over the next hill is a very old cabin, one that was here way before me. There is a hook-up for your horse outside where you throw your reins. In this cabin is a small pot-belly stove with a wooden sink and an old well that pumps water. Who- ever lived here had to haul water. It is just a one person cabin with a small wooden bunk and table to sit on. Old spice cans of mustard and celery seed, many Farmer Brothers coffee cans and cast-iron pots still hang on the walls. No curtains. No life now but definitely this person had an incredible view of the expansive Columbia River. I like sitting on the porch and looking out.

I hear someone yelling in the distance. Unusual because most people don't make this place a destination. I see a horse in the distance. No dogs. Ain't Johnny Crush. As I squint my eyes, I see a man ahead. I better get off my ass so I don't look like I'm trespassing.

"Hey there!" I wave my hat letting my brown hair fall to my shoulders.

"Hey yourself!" The man definitely sees me and speeds up to get a closer look.

"Hey, what are you up to?" A young, tanned, brown- haired, green-eyed gentleman calls out to me.

"Ah, nothing. Just out for a hike."

"You live around here?" His quizzical green eyes look up and down my body.

"Why yes I do! I live down in the ravine. The octagon house. I'm Desiree. Nice to meet you." I extend my hand out to his. He slides off his horse and wipes his hand on his shirt.

"Same here. My name is Larry. I live on the back side property. Adjacent to Bria's."

"Really?"

"Yep. I'm working on building my cabin there."

"So you're a carpenter?"

"Yep."

"Well, are you interested in helping me get my cabin back in shape? It has been neglected."

"Sure. How bout you get up on my horse and we'll take a ride on down."

"That's might kind of you, Larry."

There is something about riding on the back of a sweaty horse with a sweaty man. Riding behind a man you've just met is a bit exciting. Your arms have to go around his chest and your hands have to clutch together tight just above his navel. Then of course you have to hold on tight against his sweaty back with your sweaty chest, and conjure up the female goddesses of the woods to help you. His brown locks smell good like he washes them once in awhile and combs them. His manly odor is different than Ruby's. How can I say? Younger, fresher. Thinking about it as he whips his horse into a gallop makes my thighs a little sweatier too. Soon as we are back at Bria's road he slows his horse down to a trot.

"Is your place over there?" He points with one arm.

"Yep, over there." We trot down towards the ravine but obviously he knows the right way to go because his large thoroughbred has plenty of room to walk on a path that is familiar.

This morning I hear a noise outside my French doors. Something sounds like it is rustling back and forth. I peer through my lace curtains to see three wild turkeys pecking at the ground.

"Another beautiful day in Fruitland," I announce to the world. I jump out of bed and run over to the cook stove to light a fire to get my tea pot whistling. I run back to my bed and jump under the covers because I leave all my windows open at night and it is like a refrigerator down in the ravine. Even if it is 95 degrees out in the day, at night it will go way down to 45 or 50 degrees. Great for sleeping. I take a deep breath and snuggle a little longer with my covers.

A loud engine roars up my road. I stare out my window again as the turkeys take off and a motorcycle and a man stop about 20 feet from my cabin.

"Damn, I haven't had my gunpowder tea yet." I see that it is the young Larry hopping off his cycle.

"Shit, I don't have any clothes on!" I leap out of my bed to my duffel bag and find a sarong. I tie it in an exotic way.

"Hello, Hello!" I run to the door just as he knocks one, two and three.

"Hello, Miss Desiree. I came to take you up on your offer." My eyes crisscross at that thought. He looks at my confused response.

"Looking at your cabin?"

"Óh... Yes, yes, come on in."

"I hope I didn't wake you."

"No. I was just getting my tea on." The tea kettle sings at a high pitch. I twirl towards the stove with my sarong flip flopping every which way.

"Amazing house you built." Larry follows me into the kitchen and closes the door behind him. He notices that there are some chewed up holes in the door.

"Looks like some critters have gotten in while you were gone. Flying squirrels or mice or bats."

"Oh yes. Every Tom, Dick and Harry seems to love to play house when I am gone. Let's sit outside and drink some tea."

I don't know what's so magical about the field. Maybe because it is a circular field holding a circular house. The energy level for a circle is like a balancing mantra for me. Larry helps me unfold two sun chairs for us to sit on and we look out onto my field of waving grasses and large pines.

"Why did you leave?"

"Oh..." I chuckled. "I guess I wanted a new adventure. I met a man, got pregnant, and wanted to see what the big city had to offer."

"I heard from Johnny that you sing."

"Yes, I do. Partly because of that too. I wanted to see where my voice would take me."

"Well, it is important to listen to your voice." Larry's words float off his lips as the hot steam floats off his tea cup.

We sit for several minutes just listening to the birds chirping and the bees flying.

"Well, if you need some help on the place, let me know and I will get to work."

"Mighty nice of you to come and visit. I will definitely take you up on the offer." I keep staring at the bees. He places his cup down in my palm and tips his hat down. Then he is gone.

Hunting Honey

Later on in the heat of the day, I drive down to the honey hut to say hello to Johnny but no one is there again. I decide to go towards Hunters which is about 8.7 miles south of Fruitland. Further down past Majestic Bay road, I see a truck pulled over on the third turnout. I can see a trail going down to the river. There are rows and rows of Willow trees along a beautiful sandy beach.

No one is in sight so I throw off my clothes and jump in. The cold Columbia River in all its grandeur refreshes my eyes and body on a hot day. I swim and swim. It is completely quiet with no one in sight for miles north or south.

"This is Heaven," I shout to the blue sky as I lay on my back in the water.

"Yes it is." A familiar voice replies. I flip back over.

"Johnny? Johnny, where are you?" I am gulping water as I start to laugh.

"Desiree, welcome back to Fruitland." Johnny runs out from behind some rose bushes and plants himself on my sarong.

"Are you going to join me or not?" I holler back.

With that invitation, Johnny tears off his rough cut jeans and runs and dives down to the river towards me. Splashing water at him, he splashes back and then we begin to swim side by side. Free-styling, then back-stroking and then breast-stroking till we get tired and land back at the beach.

"Oh, I have missed you Desiree."

"Oh sweet Johnny, I have missed you too. Come

over to my towel."

Johnny plops down by my side and lies with his back against the towel and his eyes towards the open sky.

"Are you happy, Desiree?"

"Oh Johnny, there is so much I am exploring. I am working on myself, going to school, raising my beautiful boy Coyote, and trying to love Ruby lots. And you, Johnny. Are you happy?"

"Oh you know me. Me and my bees. The honey keeps flowing around here. Greater and greater amounts every year. Will you come by my honey hut and see what I've been up to?"

I turn over on my side towards him.

"Certainly I will."

We both sit up. The baking sun begins to set. Johnny pulls on his faded jeans.

"See you tomorrow."

I wrap my sarong around me and slip my feet into my thongs. Together we leave our favorite watering hole.

My Bed

After getting some veggies from the Fruitland store, I drive back to my cabin and there is Larry resting by his motorcycle.

"I thought I would talk with you about what I could do to get your cabin back in shape."

"I would love to hear what you've got to say." He takes my canvas bags of goodies and we walk over to the back door. When we get inside, he places the bags on the counter and walks towards the bed that I have set up in the living space by the French doors.

"It's getting a little dark in here." I light the kerosene lamps on the piano.

"Those are beautiful," Larry comes closer to the piano. "You play the piano, Desiree?"

"Yes I do."

"Would you play and sing me a song?" I blush and sit on the piano bench as he sits on the edge of my bed. He looks nice in his clean jeans, tight blue T-shirt and ruffled brown hair. I decide to play and sing, "Killing Me Softly." When I finish, I turn around and notice he has taken off his shirt and thrown it on my hard wood floor.

"Nice floor." His foot stops tapping.

"I got the wood from crates of old oak pallets in Spokaloo."

There is his shirt strewn across my floor. Bold as bold can be. I don't jump on him immediately. I want to peruse the terrain of his upper body. Men's bodies are not as beautiful as women's but I do like to look at their hips and shoulders. Their area of concern below their hips is not the deal-breaker. He has slender hips and his upper body is firm not bulky, just medium built like a young man. After I spend ample time looking him up and down, I pick up my red bag. The red bag is a necessity for any woman. If you are traveling alone, you can have a small vibrational item to sooth you when in need of releasing tensions and oils to coat your body that help send healing remedies to the mind.

I approach him first with the oils. I pour some into the palm of my hands and rub my hands together while he starts to unbutton his jeans. Placing my fingers to his nose, he takes a deep breath in.

"Roll over." I say.

I pull his jeans down. There is what I have been looking for. His tight brown rear end. I place my hands on his shoulders as I position my knees by his hips and squeeze gently. Massaging with deep strokes down his back, I stroke his read end down the center and up along the sides. He squirms with a motion that cannot buck me off. Placing my hands underneath his upper front thighs, I pull upwards with my hands towards his back. After a few minutes, I whisper into his left ear.

"Do you want me to stop?"

He grabs my hair and pulls me gently to his side. He flips his own body on top of mine.

"No, me first," I push my hands against his chest. "Get on your back."

I take full command of my needs and place his penis into my juicy vagina.

"Oh, my, my, my..." I start to breath at a quicker pace.

"That's the spot. Do it deeper, deeper." Then I scream like a cowgirl who had won first prize at a bucking bronco competition.

"Now it is my turn." He grabs me from behind and flips me over never letting his penis release from my vagina. He isn't much of a screamer but he is definitely transported. We lay there together for a few hours looking through the French door window as a million and one stars flicker on the Fruitland night sky.

Humming with the Hummingbirds

A glimmer of the morning sun hits my eyes and I open them to see that Larry did leave last night. Laying down for a minute longer I start to think about the night before, but it is time to get up. I brush my teeth, comb my hair and greet the day. First order of business is to see the beavers. I put on a red long-sleeve shirt and faded jeans, heavy duty boots, and my cowboy hat, and grab my machete. Walking down the ravine to the creek, I follow the water looking for beaver dams. They are chewing on my deciduous trees. Their teeth chisel beautiful trees into pointed stumps and then they drag them to make their dams. More and more trees are missing. The culvert under the dirt bridge looks like the spot where the beavers are traveling up and down. There are dams below and up above the bridge. I start whacking with my machete to loosen up a small dam by the bridge and I am successful in making that dam no longer exist. But I am thirsty and it is time to eat breakfast. There are numerous butterflies and hummingbirds following me as I walk up my road. I see a few deer dart past me as I enter the open pasture. It is a beautiful expansive morning in Fruitland. The clouds are stacked on top of each other and the sun keeps playing hide and seek with each cloud formation. There is some scat on the ground past the old water pump. It looks pretty fresh and of course it is cougar. I know he is out there because I heard him last night. Between the coyotes yelling and the cougars crying it is a wonder anyone can get a good night's sleep. The hummingbirds and butterflies circle the wild rose bushes growing by my house. I better get my hummingbird feeder up.

I've decided I'd love some zucchini bread. Pulling my Moosewood Cookbook out, I sort my ingredients of brown rice and garbanzo flour, eggs, Johnny's honey, vanilla, canola oil and dashes of allspice and cinnamon. Putting it all together, I place my old bread pans filled with batter into the cook stove. The cabin is getting warm and I make a cup of tea and start to play the piano. Thank God, my favorite Judy Collins book has not gotten chewed up by the mice Opening up the pages I pick "The Wild Mountain Thyme."

> *For the summertime is coming,*
> *And the trees are sweetly blooming,*
> *And the Wild mountain thyme,*
> *blooms around the purple heather.*
> *Will you go, laddie go?*

As I sing, "The Roads Are Coming," "The Last Thing on my Mind," and "Suzanne", I can smell the bread and I stop to check on it. It is warm and brown and I can't wait to cut into a loaf right away.

Peaches and Cream

The peaches are in and I am driving up to Ricky Creek Orchards. It is almost to Kettle Falls. I love driving up past Hunters to Cedonia, past the Gifford Ferry, then Rice, and Daisy. If Andrew Wyeth was still alive I know he would have fallen in love with the landscape of this area. It reminds me of "Christina's World." The wheat and oat field wave knee high and all you see are blue skies forever. Ricky Creek's trees are lined up near the road and they are loaded with peaches. I go into the barn that Annie, the owner has decorated with antiques.

"Hey Desiree, look who's back."

"Good to see you again, Annie. Are your peaches ready?"

"Oh yes! We had a good crop this year." Annie pulls out 20 pound boxes for me to choose from.

"Those look fabulous. I will take that one."

"Are you still living in Fruitland?"

"No, not full time. Just in the summer now."

"Well, it is still a pleasure to see you whenever you come by." I pay her and off I go to review my canning and drying skills for the summer.

A Pleasant Surprise

Luckily, before I left, I had put a little kindling in the stove. I light a match and get my dinner going. I think tonight I will fry up some broccoli, celery and onions with garbanzo beans and make a potato sauce gravy with thyme and parmesan cheese. Yummy! I light several candles around the cabin and put on Chopin Etudes. Sitting down and watching the sun set my mind wanders off to Larry. He's an interesting person but I don't get a hit off of him. He is not as soft as Ruby. When we are together, Ruby looks at my eyes a long time, and he touches my skin softly.

I'm kind of missing Ruby right now. Ruby knows more about a woman's body whereas Larry is still figuring things out. Oh well, you never know till you try. On the stove, my pot is steaming. I also notice there are some lights coming up my road. Hum, I wonder who it is? Oh my! It's Coyote and Ruby. I put on my wool coat because there is a coolness in the air and run out to greet them.

"Oh, you sweet man!" I yell as Ruby stops the car and gets out. Coyote jumps out and the both of them run over to give me a family hug. We hold each other for at least a minute and then Coyote points up at the night sky.

"Oh Ma, look at all the stars."

"Welcome to Fruitland and my cabin, Coyote."

"I've brought my hammer, skill saw, nails, leveler and my tool-belt."

"How did you know that I was thinking about you?"

Ruby smiles and opens the back door of the car

to give Coyote his sleeping bag and backpack.

"You are my sweet stuff and I needed to be by my sweet stuff." Ruby sweetly grabs me.

Coyote nudges me.

"Where do I put this Ma?"

"Let's go in. I think I have a special spot for you."

Coyote darts into the house as Ruby pulls me closer to him. He fondles my ass and rubs his front hips to my hips.

"Can't be without you for a week, you know that."

"Yes I do." I kiss him strong and long until Coyote hollers.

"Ma, I found a spot."

Coyote has found his spot. On the second floor of the cabin is an enclosed space that has a closed door. My old bedroom. The only window in it looks up into the sky and there are built-in shelves that are low to the ground. Ruby starts to munch on my peaches from Ricky Creek. I set his bag of clothes on a chair next to my bed.

"Okay everyone, help me with dinner."

Coyote takes a plate from the kitchen table.

"Mmm, my favorite Ma." I dish up a large portion of the garbanzo sauce over rice and give him a kiss.

Ruby has started on some salad. He is chopping lettuce, tomatoes, cucumbers, and green peppers and tossing them on Coyote's plate. Then I put our plates down on the table as he looks for his favorite dressing in the refrigerator.

"Where's the dressing?"

I get the olive oil, lemon and tamari out of the

refrigerator. "Sorry. You will have to settle for my homemade dressing."

"Okay." Ruby sits down and starts to eat the main course.

"Ma, I love that we all eat together."

Ruby looks up from his food as I pour some dressing on his salad.

"It has always been the most important time for me too, Coyote. Sitting down and having a nice dinner with my family or my friends is the best."

"Ma, can we come here more often? And spend fun time together?"

"Of course. Tomorrow we are going to have a great time down at Emerson's Cove. I want you to eat well and get a good night sleep." Ruby looks up at me and under the table puts his hand on my thigh. I look over at him and wink.

"Dad will get a good night's rest tonight too."

Emerson Cove

To get to Emerson's Cove, you have to take a right on Highway 25 from the Bible Camp, then down a quarter mile and on your left is a gravel road that winds down to the cove. It is where my creek, the Orapakin, meets the Columbia River. There is a beautiful bay where they meet and because the bay is not too wide or too deep the water temperature is warm. Ruby, Coyote and I lay out our assortment of beach towels and immediately take our clothes off and jump in.

"Ma, I'm going to swim across." Coyote runs down to the water's edge.

"Ok, but not without me!" I shout, chasing after Coyote. He puts his foot in and just giggles.

"Let's jump in on the count of three."

Ruby lays on the biggest beach towel watching us and then he goes back to reading "Another Roadside Attraction."

"Ma I am so glad we came to Fruitland to see you."

"You are the best surprise I could ever have. one, two, three!" I jump in and start swimming out. Coyote quickly follows me. We both rotate swimming on our tummies and backs as it is a fair distance to get to the other side. Finally we get there and take a moment to sit and look out at the expansive beauty that the river brings. I see an osprey circulating around the tops of the trees.

"Look up there Coyote. See the osprey in the top of that dead ponderosa tree." I take his small hand and lift it up where I point towards the tree.

"Point with your finger and I will help you find it. See how it moves back and forth on the wind."

"Yes, Ma I see it." Coyote points at more ospreys flying by. One of the ospreys lands back at his home on the top of the tree.

"I love it here, Ma."

"I love it here, too."

"How come we don't live here, Ma?

"Fruitland is a beautiful place to come to but it is not a place to get an education or go for your dreams."

"You have dreams, Ma. Don't you?"

"Yes, I do." I put my arm around his shoulders and pull him closer to me. We both sit quietly together looking across the river. We also see Ruby is munching on the lunch that I brought.

"Dad's eating, Ma."

"Right, I'll beat you to the other side."

"Ok, but can I get a head start?" Coyote runs towards the water and jumps in. I wait and see that he is at least 15 feet away and start to breast stroke across.

"Dad, you promised you wouldn't eat all the lunch." Ruby opens up the wooden lunch basket to reveal many tuna sandwiches that I have made. I run up and lay down on my beach towel.

"Also some apples and pickles and carrots are in there too."

Ruby has designated a center spot where he has put napkins out for the sandwiches.

"What is there to drink?"

Ruby and I both say, "Water." Coyote looks at us with a squished up mouth. I hand him a mason jar of ice water.

"Ruby, let's stop at Mary's store in Fruitland and

say hello. Maybe Mary has some apple juice for you, my little man."

After lunch we all take a nap on our individual beach towels. When I wake up I start to gather up the remaining food into my wooden lunch basket. Ruby wakes up and helps with the towels. We all get dressed and Coyote starts picking up trash on the beach, wrappers, old beer cans and plastic bottles.

"Way to go, Coyote. Trying to keep our beach beautiful."

"We've got to, Ma."

Mary's Store

Ruby starts up the station wagon with Coyote in the back and the windows down for air conditioning. Fruitland's main street consists of a convenience store and a gas station that Mary owns. Inside the store Mary operates the post office. Fruitland has about 100 people living here mostly farmers. When we open the swinging door of her store a bell jingles a high pitch and Mary looks up from the back of the counter.

"Why if it isn't Desiree!" Mary runs from behind the counter and gives me a big bear hug. "Is this Ruby and your son?"

"Yes they are. Oh Mary, you are a sight for sore eyes." Mary is about fifty years old with a short brown bob haircut.

"I am so happy you came back. I've just got a letter for you but I didn't know where to forward it to," Mary hands me a letter marked:

> *Desiree*
> *Fruitland, WA.*

"It is amazing that it got here to you." Mary points to the address.

"Not too many people can boast about getting mail by a first name and just the little town we live in."

"Bet you couldn't return it either, Mary. It just says Big Paul Skinny." Ruby points to the return address. Mary chuckles.

"Yep, I was wondering and hoping you'd come back at some point."

"Oh my God! Big Paul Skinny. Remember I told you about him? I traded that Camaro for the 1949 pickup truck so he could go to Los Angeles."

"You go outside and read it while Coyote and I pick out some cool shirts and hats with Fruitland emblems on them."

"Ruby, I want this one!" Coyote picks out a blue sweat shirt with six running wild turkeys printed all over it.

I walk through the front door as the little bell rings and I sit down on one of the carved black bear benches. Savoring this moment, I tear the letter open and see large flowery writing.

> *Dear Desiree*
> *I know it has been a long time since I connected with you. But I've been doing really well in Los Angeles. Every time I take your white Camaro out on the highways I think of you. I loved the times that we sang together. The music business has been good to me and I was hoping that you might want to come down and record on my next album that will be coming out next year. Your voice blends so well with mine. What do you say to that?*
> *Call me. 310-753-8195*
> *Big Paul Skinny*

"Oh my God!" I put the letter to my chest. The chance to go to Los Angeles and record. Maybe I could do some acting too. I wonder how Ruby will feel about me leaving. We'd have to figure out Coyote's schedule. I know it can work. I can make this work.

Suddenly the little bell rings and the door opens and Coyote runs over to me.

"Ma, look what I got." Coyote is wearing a dark blue Fruitland trucker hat and the matching sweatshirt with wild turkeys running all over it.

"Don't you look amazing." Coyote smiles and sit by me as Ruby walks out of the store with three cold bottles of apple juice.

"Hey... apple juice? What did Big Paul Skinny have to say?" Ruby sits down and hands me a bottle. I snuggle close to Ruby's side.

"Ruby, let's go back to the cabin. I've got some news."

"Desiree, you know I don't like secrets." Ruby pulls away from me.

"Okay, okay. I will tell you on the way back."

Los Angeles

Ruby jumps into the driver seat as Coyote buckles up in the back. I roll down the window and watch the scenery of crumbling barns whizz by. I really want this but I know Ruby has his job to do and he will have to do more work with the running of the house and taking care of Coyote. As we turn right on Lake Mudgett road, I look at Ruby.

"Ruby, Big Paul Skinny wants me to come to Los Angeles to record with him."

"When?" Ruby drives up the gravel road towards the Gramers. "Everyone roll up the windows." Coyote and I roll up the windows quickly before the dust of the road tries to get in the car. I wonder if he thinks we are all going to Los Angeles.

"Ruby, I might have to go by myself." Ruby slows the car down. I look ahead to see what could be slowing us down.

"How long are you going to be gone?"

"I don't know."

"Desiree, I will miss you. But you have to do this. This is a great opportunity." Ruby keeps his eyes on the road.

I look at Ruby and feel so excited that he is excited.

"Coyote and I can handle it. Besides I've got my job and our little man has to go to school. But we will miss you."

Looking over my shoulder and seeing that Coyote has fallen asleep in the backseat, I am feeling really blessed. I extend my hand onto Ruby's upper leg and squeeze it. Ruby looks at me and smiles.

Then we continue past the honey hut and across the creek up to the cabin road.

When we get to the cabin, I get out and open the back door and unlock Coyote's seat belt. He is still asleep and I lower his head so his whole body is resting on the back seat. Ruby comes up from behind.

"Let him sleep a little longer. We can have our summer afternoon delight."

I put my arms on Ruby's shoulders. "Ruby, I love you so much. Do you know that?"

Ruby takes my hand and we walk towards the cabin. When we open the door, Ruby quickly takes off his jeans. I take off my sarong and we both stand there naked. Ruby puts one hand on the back of my head and draws me close to his face kissing me softly on the forehead, eyes, cheeks, nose, upper lip, lower lip and neck. Then he kisses my shoulders, my breasts and travels down to my navel and pubic bone. My vagina can't stand it.

"Come to bed now." Ruby stands up.

"Okay, but I want you now, Ruby."

I lay down on my make-shift bed and Ruby rubs his penis with his spit and inserts himself inside me. Gently moving back and forth a little at a time, he then blows air into my ears to get me more excited.

"Oh, I love the way you feel inside of me."

"Me too."

"Let me get on top."

"On one condition. Can we roll over and keep me inside?"

He grins.

"Okay, One, two, three go!"

We hold each other tight just like a peanut

butter and honey sandwich rolling to the right and positioning me on top.

"Oh, let's add that to our special skills." Ruby laughs.

I lift my upper body and sit down deeper on Ruby. He waits for me as I close my eyes and concentrate on the special spot of release.

"Oh, that's the spot. Don't stop." I orgasm once, twice, thrice and on the fourth orgasm I scream really loud.

"Shhhh. Coyote will hear you."

"You next." I laugh and roll onto my back.

"Lift your legs up and wrap them hard around my back." I do exactly as he commands and soon Ruby comes for a very long time. Ruby is a quiet comer, but his eyes roll back into his head as I rub upwards on his upper thighs. Then I take my hands and run my fingers in his hair pulling the ends up to the ceiling. To top it off, I pull the top of his ears upwards.

"Oh, I love you. I love you so much."

Ruby rolls off of me and lays on his back.

"Close your eyes for a quick nap, my sweets." I kiss his face and suddenly Coyote pushes the door open and yells.

"Where are you guys?"

"We are over here." I wave to Coyote. He runs onto the bed and cuddles between the two of us.

"You smell, Ma."

"Yes, I do," I laugh and smell my underarms. "Let's wash off."

While Ruby takes a nap, I fill a pot of water and get it boiling on the stove. I pour the water into a 5 gallon bucket and mix it with cold water from the creek. I place some plastic sun chairs outside and put the bucket in front of the chairs. I find my bar of Soap Lake soap and Korean glove scrubbers.

"Here is a yogurt container. Dip it in the water and dump the water on your body. Then start scrubbing with the gloves and this bar of soap." I hand the container, gloves and soap to Coyote.

As the sun starts to set, Coyote and I clean our armpits and areas of concern while the swallows fly over our heads catching mosquitoes.

Fixing Fruitland

The next morning, I open my eyes and see Ruby sitting in the rocking chair looking at the ceiling of the cabin. Just rocking and staring at the corners of the walls. I turn over and look at Coyote nestled by the heat stove. His sleeping bag completely covers his body and his head.

"What are you doing, Ruby?" I whisper.

"Desiree, your place needs some help."

"Yes it does. And since you're here I was thinking we could do a few things. But we can't forget to play."

Ruby gets up out of his chair and bends down to kiss me on my forehead.

"By the way, I met this Larry guy. He said he might be interested in helping bring the cabin back to life." I lift the flannel covers off my naked body and walk over to the cook stove to start a fire. Grabbing my sarong, Ruby walks over to the counter and wraps it around me. Ruby finds his coffee filter and scoops some ground coffee beans into the filter.

"Sounds good to me."

"Do eggs and turkey bacon sound good too? Fresh from Darlene's farm."

I place my iron skillet on the stove and add olive oil to the pan and start frying. Coyote loves the smell of turkey bacon. As soon as it starts sizzling, Coyote unzips his sleeping bag and runs over with the sandman shining in his eyes.

"Did you sleep well?" I wipe the sand from his inner eyes.

"Ma, I slept well. Can I have some breakfast

now?"

"Get the plates on the table and silverware. Do you want some hot cocoa?"

"Yes, yes, yes." Coyote sees the camping utensils in a yogurt container and picks 3 forks, 3 spoons, and 3 knives and places them correctly on the table. He obviously has been watching me. Julia Childs would be proud of him.

"Here are the plates."

Coyote carefully takes the plates from my hands and puts them down. Then he sits down. I am stirring Johnny's honey into a saucepan with fair trade cocoa and milk. I put my fingers into the saucepan and it is the perfect temperature. Not too hot and not too cold.

"Here you go." I pour the hot cocoa into a green mug and he sips a little at a time.

"The eggs are sunny side up today, sir."

"Thanks ma, and yummy cocoa."

I dish up eggs and browned turkey bacon onto a plate and serve it to Coyote. Ruby places some homemade raisin bread into the toaster. We all sit down and look out of the windows where the hummingbird feeder is. Watching the birds flit by and listening to Vince's classical radio station playing quietly in the background, I realize how happy I am.

"How about we go to my special cave today?"

Everyone looks up from their plates.

"It's on the way to Larry's and then you and he can talk, Ruby."

Visiting

After breakfast, we get our hiking boots on, long shirts and pants, hats and sunscreen. There are ticks in Washington but not the kind with Lyme disease. Still they are here. It is a hot day as the temperature is rising to 95 degrees and just the thought of dipping my feet in the cold spring water seems like a great idea. We climb up the hill to Bria's.

"The trail has been taken over by the rose bushes again."

"Back away. I'll clear a pathway." Ruby starts slashing at the bushes with the machete. As we near a cliff of large rocks, I signal to Ruby to stop.

"Duck real low and follow me through these thick elderberry trees. There is a group of large granite rocks up ahead."

"Ma, I see the cave. There it is."

"Shh! Promise you will never let anyone know. Before you enter, you have to say a prayer of thanks." Coyote bows his head.

"Thank you cave."

By the side of the opening of the cave, I have stacked flat rocks on top of each other. Large at the bottom to the smallest at the top. Also I have put dried flowers of yarrow and shooting stars.

"Follow me." We disappear into the cave. As we slide our bodies through the narrow cave opening, the smell of wet earth becomes intoxicating. Coyote turns on his head lamp and now the cave is lit up. Ruby pulls out a large candle and I light it as we both feel the excitement for Coyote. In front of his eyes is a large space that has a wide basin of still water. The basin can comfortably hold four people. We place the candle on a carved out ledge.

"This is way cool, ma and pa."

Ruby has already taken off his clothes and now is sliding down into the smooth basin. Coyote follows Ruby and then I help Coyote to make sure he is safe.

"How did you find this place?" Ruby asks.

"I found this spring by the creek and followed where the source was coming from. When I was poking around the ground and rocks, I uncovered the cave."

"Coyote, If you put your foot here, you can stand on the top of a flat rock."

Ruby starts to lift his body out and sits on the side of the basin.

"I still prefer Lake Mudgett or Roosevelt."

Coyote reaches out his arms to Ruby. Ruby lifts him up to his chest and holds him close.

"Dad, your lips are turning blue."

"How about after visiting Larry we go to warm up at Lake Mudgett?"

Larry's house is further up the road after Bria's. It is a dusty road and it passes an abandoned farm with old tractors and assorted junk cars parked every which way. Old fences are partially standing and partially fallen down. As you pass the farm-house you begin to see unusual signs at the gate of his road.

Do not pass here! I will shoot.

"Larry seems a little paranoid," Ruby says.

"I don't think there's a problem. He seems like a nice guy to me."

Coyote just keeps trucking down the road not

even noticing or caring about the signs. Larry is outside working on an generator. He sees us and takes off his hat and waves it.

"Hey Larry." I smile at him but he keeps his face very neutral.

"Hey." Ruby interrupts.

"This is my old man, Ruby, and my son, Coyote."

As Ruby extends his hand to Larry, Coyote extends his hand. Larry takes off his gloves and shakes Coyote's hand and then Ruby's.

"Desiree says you are a carpenter. We were wondering if you might do some work on the place. Button it up so that the mice and flying squirrels and bats don't get in."

"I do need some extra work." He wipes his forehead with his shirt sleeve. "Would be glad to."

"Great," Ruby and I both chime in.

"We'll leave you a list of things to do. How about $15.00 an hour?"

"Sounds fine." Larry nods his head.

"Well, best not keep you from your work here." Ruby shakes Larry's hand and then Larry extends his hand to me.

"Thank you for everything." I shake Larry's hand.

"Mr. Larry, thank you too." Coyote shakes his other hand.

After days of eating well, sleeping ten hours a night, swimming in Lake Mudgett and Roosevelt, and playing cards till the wee hours, we pack up the station wagon to go back to the Emerald City. Ruby drives back with Coyote and I take my car following and holding up the back of the caravan. We stop to say farewell to the Columbia River at Fort Spokane with a final dip. Then we drive back on Highway 25 towards Creston. I turn on the classical radio station as I turn right on Highway 2 but the static soon begins to wipe out Vince's melodious voice. I turn off the radio and start thinking about school but then I start thinking about Big Paul Skinny's offer. I can't wait to get back and talk to him about the dates. I don't know how the head of the department is going to take this. What if they say I am out of the program? Damn. I try to think of some positive outcome.

More Choices

I walk into Cornish. After my break, I am open for whatever the teachers have planned. Big Paul Skinny is in the pre-production part of the project. He wants me in Los Angeles in two months. He will be sending me the music and score. Lena Swift passes by me as I walk to my first class, stage combat.

"You're looking different."

"Oh, I am. I am re-energized." I say as I give her a wave with my hand.

"Look at the bulletin board. There is a gift for you." Lena waves back.

Whatever does she mean? I turn the corner and notice many of my classmates looking at the board.

"Congratulations, Desiree!" many of them shout out.

"How did you manage that?" Sarah points at the board.

"What?" I stop dead in my tracks, suspicious.

"You have the lead in *The Cherry Orchard*." Sarah comes through the crowd and shakes my shoulders.

"Oh my God. It can't be real."

"It's real, alright."

"When does it open?"

"In five weeks and then it runs for two weekends."

I am quickly figuring out the time line of Big Paul Skinny project and this new project. He wants me in Los Angeles in two months. It is going to work out.

"It is going to work," I repeat out loud to myself.

"Of course it is going to work. You will be

wonderful in the role." Sarah gives me a hug.

After the first day of classes I drive home and open the door to see Coyote and Ruby sitting on the couch. I take off my backpack heavy with books and note-pads and unbutton my coat.

"Guess what?"

"What?" Ruby gets up and enters the kitchen to start unpacking a bag of groceries.

"I just got the lead role in *The Cherry Orchard*."

"Chekhov. Amazing."

Coyote moves over as I lay the long way on the couch. I put my feet up on the arm. Ruby comes over and takes off my shoes. Coyote sits on the floor next to my head.

"Ma, way to go."

"You guys, I have a lot of work to do on this play and getting ready for Big Paul Skinny. I am feeling that I might let you down because I will be at school late and on the weekends. Plus I will be trying to learn the singing parts for Big Paul."

"Have you told the head of the theatre department yet?" Ruby takes off my socks and starts to rub my feet.

"Not yet."

"Desiree, they should know."

"Oh... not yet. Not till the right moment. I don't want to jeopardize the role."

"Smart thinking." Ruby rubs my right foot so deep that I am feeling a pain in my foot but I don't care. "You will figure it out."

"Oh yes. I will figure it out."

Stay Immersed

For the next five weeks, the cast is immersed in *The Cherry Orchard*. I love my role as Lyubov Ranevskaya. I am connecting to Ranevskaya on the sadness of her son's death. It is so painful to think of losing Coyote.

The preliminary blocking has been mapped out for us. The costume designer has shown me beautiful dresses she is designing. The set designer has created a simple set with white tree in the background behind sheer white floor length curtains. There are some quick costume changes but I am told there will be crew people backstage to help me. Between the practices after school, I haven't been home for dinner till later then we usually plan. Coyote doesn't seem to mind as the Learning Tree provides a child supervisor for the parents who can't pick them up till 6:00 p.m. Ruby and I take turns picking him up. When I get home I always notice their adventurous time making dinner. Krusteaz crepes with crème of mushroom soup or Krusteaz pancakes with crème of tuna, Krusteaz tortillas with beans and rice or Krusteaz biscuits with tomato soup.

Big Paul Skinny sent a large envelope today. It has a cassette of the music and lyric sheets with chords. I haven't heard his voice in a while. He sounds better on the cassette tape than I remember. He has recorded his part and then my part. It looks like I am singing on the whole album. The songs are so like him: the kind of songs you would love to hear on a long road trip. Reminds me of Gordon Lightfoot. I am instantly in love with all of the songs and constantly singing my part while I am making dinner of lentil loaf with mushrooms and cheese, eggplant Parmesan with homemade tomato sauce, and gado-gado with peanut and coconut sauce.

Keep Breathing

The opening night of *The Cherry Orchard*. The gym has been transformed into a beautiful but simplistic Russian landscape. My costumes feel luxurious on me. Lace trimmings around the collar and wrist are interwoven with sky blue velvet ribbons. Herringbone has been sewn into the midriff to create the illusion an even smaller waistline than I already have. I have been practicing wearing my special made-to-order corset. I am tied in so tightly that I can barely breathe. But adding more shallow-breathing to my already shallow breathing character is perfect. The cast has been practicing so hard and I feel that I have melded my life with that of Lyubov Ranevskaya. She is a complicated mother. In many ways her aristocratic status is not what I would naturally gravitate to.

The importance of this evening lies with the fact that our show is being judged. In other words, we are in a competition. I don't know the details-or rather I can't be bothered with the details. Right at this very moment, the lights are going down and I need to make my fleeting entrance. As soon as I cross the stage, I will need to do that quick costume change. I come in taking in the old orchard, our home, our old friends and servants. I breathe in deeply and enter. The audience has quieted down and I see through Ranevskaya's eyes and feel the emotions of surprise, regret, and delight of all my surroundings, and then I go off stage. In the dark, crew members are rushing to take off my hat, my gloves, my cape, new top, new skirt, new shoes, make sure my hair stays in its coiffure. My heart is pounding. My top has to be buttoned at the cuffs and I can hear the lines from the other actors. I know the cue line is coming up very soon now and the crew is still not getting me completely put together. Oh my God, the line is coming and I have to go. I am slapping hands away.

"I have to go!" I whisper. I am practically grabbing at my skirt to make sure it is staying up. I have no idea what I look like but I can't leave the other actors on stage trying to cover up for me not entering on time. So I enter. I breathe a little bit deeper and hope there is no costume malfunction. I sit and reminisce about the old days and laughingly dismiss what others are saying and what they want me to do. I am joyous to be back home. The cherry orchard means so much to our family. I cannot bear for the orchard to be cut down.

As the second act unfolds, my life is being exposed, my lover in Paris who is sending me telegrams wants me back. He has been robbing me and has left me before which caused me to be suicidal. For a moment I speak about the loss of my husband, my son, and my cherry orchard. I am sitting on a bench and in my imagination, I am not able to face the truths. Lyubov, my name, means "love" in Russian and I have exemplified my love with generosity and kindness. In the play, I feel that I am continuously fleeing from both Paris and Russia. I am like a bird fluttering and can't seem to stay long in any situation. Memories, so many memories of the past prevent me from moving onto a better life. Seeing the orchard delivers so much happiness and when I think about Fruitland and its nature I speak with so much passion. The play ends and we all take our bows. I feel good about my performance. There was the wardrobe incident but I stayed focused and present with my character's life on stage. The energy off stage is upbeat and everyone congratulate each other. It will be wonderful to hear what my teachers think. There is much more I can learn.

"See you on Monday for notes," Bill says shaking everyone's hands. I am feeling nervous now because I have to tell the department that I am leaving. I know I have put it off, but I didn't want to jeopardize this role.

"See you Monday, Bill!" I wave and smile.

How am I going to tell them about leaving? I could just walk up to Bill Bergman office and open the door and say, "I'm leaving," then quickly shut his door and run down the hallway and leave. Run out the front door of the building, get into my Dodge Dart and drive home. Or I could just never show up for classes. Which is the worst way because I would flunk and then that wouldn't leave a good recommendation for future studies. Maybe the best way is to schedule a time with Bill and say:

"Bill, I have been approached by an artist in Los Angeles to record an album with him. It is a wonderful opportunity and you know that life is full of missed opportunities and I don't want to miss this one. What this means is that I will need to leave the program for a few months. I have no idea if you could grant me a sabbatical. I will return to finish the program. Your skills and knowledge as educators has been amazing and I don't want to lose that opportunity for my acting."

It sounds very professional and thoughtfully worked out and I think I will memorize it like a monologue so I don't appear like a blithering idiot. And I need to make sure I am only going to meet with Bill, not Lena or Sissy Cort. They would intimidate me.

The Talk

Monday, I arrive at school and find Bill Bergman's cubby. I put a note in saying:

> *Dear Bill*
> *I would like to talk to you privately today after school about 2:30 p.m.*
> *Thanks, Desiree*

This morning I have Alexander Technique with Margaret Nillson. She has each person sit in a chair. Then she touches certain parts of people's bodies to release their individual tensions. After relaxation has set in, she lifts each person out of their chair by the forehead and top crania of their body. It really is relaxing and when she lifts me up. I feel as light as a hummingbird feather fluttering across the room by leading with my forehead and the top of my crania.

After that class I see Bee Murphy for stage makeup. I love this class, especially when I demonstrate scars and gashes on people's faces. I did that to Coyote for Halloween. When Ruby came back from work, he screamed as Coyote acted like he had been stuck by a villain. Ruby really was mad at us. I guess I am pretty good at this class. People say it looks real.

The next class is History of Acting with Clifford Cort. He is a kind old fella who tells us all about actors and acting from the Greeks to the Romans, Middle Ages to Shakespeare, Elizabethan to modern times. One great idea that he wants me to do is to perform a solo show about a great artist.

"Clifford, how about Maria Callas?"

"Wonderful. Do it!"

"Ok, next week?"

"Go for it."

After class I will start reading as much as I can on Maria and start writing a 45-minute show about her life, her lovers, Aristotle Onassis and her passion for the opera. I have been learning "Casta Diva" from Bellini's Norma so that I will show off my voice as well as my acting. Next week I will perform it at lunchtime in the cafeteria. It will stun them. The class is ending and now I will march over to Bill's office. It is 2:30 p.m. Time to do it. Time to muster up the courage. I am walking down the hall to his door. I knock. He is not there.

"Damn." I say.

But just as I turn to leave, I see him running down the hall.

"Desiree, I am here. Don't go!"

"Hey Bill. Thanks so much for letting me speak with you."

Bill unlocks his door and opens it. There is enough room for his desk to fit and two chairs opposite each other. It reminds me of a ski chalet with its pointed roof line. Behind his desk is a large round window revealing a gray, rainy day. Bill takes off his leather shoulder bag which I know has his writings. Bill is a playwright. He is very dedicated to his craft. As well as being the chair of the theater department, he teaches playwriting. In his class, he makes my mind work. I look at scenes differently now because he keeps pestering me to ask questions why? Why am I saying this? What am I doing? And he has introduced me to the "to do" list: to provoke, to challenge, to gossip, to delight, to everything, the list is endless. His mind is very analytical. My mind is very intuitive. I work from inside what the character is feeling.

I am feeling quiet all of a sudden. I like Bill Bergman. He is Jewish like Ruby. He motions me to sit.

"Well, what brings you here today?"

I smile and look directly into his eyes.

"Bill, I have this great opportunity that has just presented itself. You know that I am a singer and I am adding my acting skill by going to school here. I know I am new to this program and I love it very much. But a singing friend of mine has asked me to come to L.A. and sing on his album. It will be sooner than later and I may need to leave for a couple of months."

Bill's forehead lines are starting to show.

"What can we do to make this happen without me getting kicked out of the program?"

Bill's forehead lines relax and I can tell he is actually thinking of a solution.

"Humm, Desiree, this is tough."

"I know, I know, I know."

"I think I will need the weekend to consider what you are asking and see if we can figure out a solution."

"Wow, that sounds promising."

"I am not going to promise anything."

"Okay, Bill, but I know you will figure out a way. I will see you on Monday."

Bill stands up and extends his hand to me. I extend my hand and shake it and look into his eyes.

"Thank you, Bill. I really appreciate you!" I gather up my backpack, coat, and hat and walk out the door. Shutting it behind me, I stand for a minute.

"Oh my God! Please help him to think of a

way." I run out of the front door of Cornish and look up to see a bunch of red and blue balloons flying upwards towards the blue sky.

A Family Meeting

The black shiny table has three place mats on it. I've also placed Johnny Crush's long honey candles in holders and lit them. The soundtrack of "The Harder They Come, The Harder They Fall" by Jimmy Cliff plays in the background. Cooking in my oven is Ruby and Coyote's favorite tofu casserole of sunflower seeds, miso, mushrooms, onions, broccoli and cheddar cheese. Basmati rice simmers on the stove top. Small salad plates of spring mix lettuce, onions, cukes, organic tomatoes and peppers rest on the place mats. I am ready to talk about the reality of me leaving now. Tonight I am going to have the final talk about it. The back door flies open.

"Mom, mom, we're home." Coyote says as he takes off his shoes and slides into his Mickey Mouse slippers. He hangs up his backpack and hands me several papers consisting of drawings and homework that he has done at school. Ruby follows, hanging up his rugged Carhartt jacket and his Fruitland trucker's hat and taking off his muddy Red Wing boots on the floor.

"Oh, hey. How was your day, Ruby?" I quickly turn off the oven and run to give him a hug.

"Oh...now that you're in my arms, fine and dandy." Ruby kisses me sweetly on the lips.

"Ma, what's for dinner?" Coyote calls from the table already munching on his salad.

"Your favorite." I walk back into the kitchen and put on my red oven mitts and pull out the casserole.

Taking it to the table, I grab a large wooden spoon and scoop some on his plate and then Ruby's and mine. Ruby sits down and grabs some dressing. Pouring a generous amount, he offers me some.

"Coyote, want some dressing?"

"Maybe when I have seconds. I am so hungry, Dad."

"Well that's good. What did you do today?"

"Vinnie had us work on reading words and writing our name and learning math with pegs."

"Did you do some art?"

"No art today, art tomorrow."

Ruby sits back in his chair and sighs.

"What did you do today, Ruby?"

"Len had us start a survey project on a piece of property in Kent. It looks like it is a subdivision. All those beautiful trees are being mowed down for more housing."

"You must be exhausted."

"I am. Lots of cutting through brush and the ground was pretty muddy."

We all eat in silence for a while.

"Listen you two, I told the drama department about my leaving."

"You're leaving, Ma? Are you going back to Fruitland again?" Coyote looks up from his plate.

"Oh no, not Fruitland Coyote. Los Angeles."

"Disneyland?" Coyote stops chewing.

Ruby gently places his hand on mine.

"Coyote, you and I are going to be holding down the fort while your Ma goes away."

"Can we go visit? I've always wanted to go to Disneyland."

"That sounds like a great idea. But we have to see if it will work out with everyone's schedule."

Coyote lifts his plate up and I give him another helping of his favorite casserole.

"Is Dad going to be cooking when you're gone?"

Ruby chuckles. "Yes, I am. You are going to learn about Krusteaz's. Krusteaz's pancake mix is the special ingredients for crepes, pancakes and biscuits. And then there is Campbell's Cream of Mushroom Soup..."

Coyote's face looks terrified. I squeeze his hand.

"Oh, I promise I will also make some meals and freeze them so you won't forget your ma's cooking."

"Yippee! But Dad it's okay if you teach me your special way of cooking too."

A Decision

On Monday morning when I arrive at Cornish, I race to my cubby to see if there is a note from Bill.

> *Desiree-*
> *Come to my office before your first class.*
> *Bill*

Bill sits at his desk finishing his comments on students homework while I sit, taking the cap on and off of my favorite writing pens. Finally he looks up and smiles. I am feeling Wow! A smile. Could that be good news? But he adjusts his glasses on his nose.

"Desiree, a few months is hard to cover up. The school has class regulations on what percentage of time that you have to put in for completion of a class. If you miss classes because you are sick..."

"Can't I make it up?"

"Yes, for some classes. But how can you make up classes for Le Coq?"

"I don't know. Could I approach Lena myself about it?"

"You certainly could ask your teachers but what if someone says no?"

"Hmm, that could clench the deal. Would that mean I would lose all that time and money and have to start over again?"

"Yes. You would have to take those classes over again."

"And since they are winter-to-spring classes, I would have to wait till the next term that they are offered?"

Bill bites his lip and nods his head in an

affirming yes.

"Okay, Bill. I am going to every head teacher. If I can get them on board, will you give me the ok?"

"Yes."

"I will do it."

I get up and grab my backpack and slam the door behind me. Looking down the corridor, I pull out a piece of paper and write down two lists. The 'Hard to Say Yes' teachers and the 'Not Hard to Say Yes' teachers. Lena Swift is first on the list. Then Sissy Cort joins her on the Hard list and Grace May on the Not Hard list. Lena I know will be staging a huge production of Hildegard with St. James Cathedral. I bet if I tell her that I will help her on the project she will say yes. Grace May is the one teacher that I am sort of sure of. The best approach I think is to be honest and sincere with her. Sissy Cort works with the mental health community. Maybe I can contribute my time to help her with the role-playing sessions that she does.

The first stop is Lena.

Observing Lena is in itself the art of LeCoq. She can hear me as I make my request, but she does not respond verbally. Her physicality tells me that she is deep in thought, as she is gathering up her duffel bags and starts to leave for the door. With a neutral face, she looks at me and opens the door.

"I will leave my response with Bill."

Frozen in time as she closes the door, I ask myself why it is so difficult for some people to communicate with words.

The next stop is Grace. Grace, will be in the cafeteria. I run down the stairs to the other side of the building. I see her sitting at a round table looking out of the bay windows. I go over to a counter of coffee and tea and get a cup of tea for myself. A table of cream, milk, nonfat milk, soy milk, sugar and napkins are by her table.

"Hey, Grace." I pour some cream into my English Breakfast tea. "Mind if I join you?"

"Sure, Desiree."

I sit down next to her and look out of the windows noticing there is a sliver of sunshine trying to seep in.

"Grace, I just spoke to Bill and he and I decided to ask my teachers how would they solve my dilemma. Knowing some of your war stories as a performing artist and the missed opportunities you've expressed, I thought you would be a great mentor to me about this situation."

Grace looks at me with the open face of a counselor. A loving, nurturing, non-judgmental counselor.

"I have this great opportunity to sing on an album in Los Angeles. What if that would mean that I would need to leave the program for a few months?"

"When?" Grace takes a sip of her cup of coffee.

"In a few weeks."

"That is a quick decision." She places the cup down. "Do you want this opportunity?"

"Yeah."

"Even if you have to leave your family, and the program with us?"

"Yes, but Bill said if I could get my head teachers to say yes, then I could make it up to all of you."

Grace pauses for a moment looking out at the tall evergreens swaying in the wind.

"Do it. I say yes. Don't make this a missed

opportunity."

"Oh my God." Tears are starting to fill up in my eyes. "Oh my God. I cannot tell you how happy you have made me. I will do anything to make up the time I have missed in your classes."

"I believe in you, Desiree."

I am taken aback by that comment. I guess I have never gotten a hit off of her. She gets up with her tray of food and I sit dumbfounded.

Sissy Cort sits in the library gathering up her many books on monologues and scene study. Her brown hair is coiffured around her studious face. I clear my throat. She turns around and sees me standing a few feet away. Her face never has a smile on it. She is a self-made woman to the highest degree. I stare at her as she stares at me. If I could ever be in that famous moment at the OK Corral wondering which cowboy is going to shoot the fastest, it would be now.

"Sissy, could I speak to you for a moment?"

Sissy looks down at her wrist-watch and thinks.

"I have about 15 minutes and then I need to pick up Clifford."

"Certainly." I motion to chairs near a corner of the library that are deserted.

"Sissy, I have an important decision to make and I need your help. I consider you a mentor."

"I never thought you considered me a mentor."

"Well, I do. I admire you in many ways. You have been hard on me and I know why. It is because you respect me and want me to be the best at what I can do. I thank you for that."

"Thank you, Desiree."

"I have been asked to sing on an album in Los

Angeles. As you well know my talents as a singer have been stronger than my acting. That is why I came to study at Cornish. With your help, I am now beginning to strengthen my talents in acting."

"I am glad you have observed this."

"I need to leave the program before it is finished to do this and Bill said I needed your permission in order to not have to start over. What can I do for you to help me?"

Sissy's eyes study my face for several minutes as I breathe deeply. I can feel my heart-beat heavy with each new intake. Sissy looks at her watch.

"I have to go to pick up Clifford." She gets up from her seat.

"Please help me. I could help you with your role playing at the mental hospital. I will do extra credit and any other homework that you feel necessary to assign. This is important to me. As you have always said, "Singing is just like acting.""

"I will let Bill know tomorrow what I have decided."

"Thank you for your time."

The funny thing is that I would have loved to have given her a hug right now, but she is not that kind of person. Clifford is. All I can ask of myself is to be still inside. To have nobility. Stand as an equal to her. I believe she expects that of me. She always says, "Know your worth."

> *Bill*
> *I talked to everyone, Grace, Lena and Sissy.*
> *They said that they will let you know by*
> *tomorrow morning. Please leave their*

*responses in my cubby tomorrow. I really
appreciate this.
Desiree*

Coyote's Decision

When I open the door at The Learning Tree, Coyote stands there with his lunch bag and backpack raring to go. He runs towards me and gives me a big old hug.

"Missed you, sweet thing."

"Me too, Ma. Let's get out of here." Coyote takes my hand and we walk out into the sunshine. "Can we go to the co-op? I am hungry, Ma."

"Me too."

At the 12th Street Co-op, Coyote and I decide it is a beans and rice kind of night. Coyote takes off towards a shelf to find two cans of pinto beans. I scoop up some basmati rice from a round barrel. Coyote runs over to the vegetables and picks out two avocados, a large head of lettuce, two tomatoes, and a cuke while I find some cans of chilies and olives.

"I want some sour cream and cheese on it too, Ma."

"This will be a feast."

Gathering up our bags, we drive home. Coyote is munching on some string mozzarella cheese. I graze on cashews. We are quiet watching the world go by.

"Ma, when are you leaving?"

"In a few weeks."

"I am going to miss you."

"I am going to miss you too."

"But I know you will be happy. I could see that on your face today when you picked me up."

"I am happy." We drive up the street and take a left at 19th and pull up to our house on Jefferson

Street. "Thank you my little man. I love you."

I have made up my mind. I am going to L.A. The present is now. There is no past. No future. From now on I am just looking at what the universe has presented to me and grabbing hold of it. I am my own person. I have dreams that are strong inside of me. If this is what I should be doing, then it will be easy. Everything will work out the way it is suppose to be. I will be able to deal with what the universe gives me.

In my dreams, I will return to Coyote and Ruby. I would never leave them for good. I love them. And Ruby and Coyote love and support me. We are a family, now. They have given me the gift to go forward. And like Fruitland, they will be there happily waiting for me.

Keep breathing. Keep listening to the sounds and silences around you. Open your eyes now. See the world with fresh eyes. Watch what will happen with a quiet mind.

ACKNOWLEDGMENTS

Thank you to Ralph Levin, Wolf Carr-Levin, Stacy Delong, Matilda Beezy, Jan Maher, Elizabeth Garfield, Imelda Daranciang, Suzy Irwin, Deanna Carter, Kelly Wimmer.

AUTHOR'S BIO

Susan Carr is a professional actress and singer performing in New York, Los Angeles and Seattle. Her film/TV credits include Lynn Shelton's *Laggies*, Mike Mill's *The Architecture of Reassurance*, Rob Devor's *ZOO*, Paul Sorvino's *That Championship Season*, *The Practice* and *Gilmore Girls*. Susan has written many plays/screenplays that have been performed at Seattle Fringe Festivals, Bumbershoot and New City's New Works Festival. Susan is the vocal coach to many Grammy nominated bands such as Macklemore, Alice in Chains, Alien Ant Farm, Mastodon and new up and coming bands, Hey Marseilles, and Pickwick. Susan teaches "The Art of Screaming!" *The Ballad of Desiree* is Susan's first novel. www.susanmcarr.com